PRAISE FOR *A WOM...*

"Marc Levy is a virtuoso of the imagination . . . This is his most beautiful romantic comedy. It's enchanting . . . a delight on every level."
—Pierre Vavasseur, *Le Parisien* (five-star review)

"A love story, a wonderful read."
—France Inter

"The beautiful tale of two people who were never meant to meet . . . Unputdownable . . . very well done."
—*Cosmopolitan*

"An action-packed New York comedy."
—Bernard Lehut, RTL

"Guaranteed to be a summer bestseller . . . It sparkles like champagne and calls to mind films like *Notting Hill.*"
—AFP

"An irresistible, sparkling comedy."
—Valérie Trierweiler, *Paris Match*

"Irresistible! You're riveted by the characters from start to finish."
—TV5Monde

"A joyful, original novel with such endearing characters. An ode to diversity."
—Europe 1

"A wonderful comedy . . . in which anything can happen."
—*Le Figaro*

"A novel both powerful and fragile. The perfect romantic comedy à la Blake Edwards."

—Elle

"A sure hit. This wonderful novel is an emotional elevator, with Marc Levy the perfect operator at the commands."

—M6 News Bulletin

"A deeply human romantic comedy."

—Le Journal de Quebec

"A love letter to New York."

—RMC

A WOMAN LIKE HER

A WOMAN LIKE HER

A Novel

MARC LEVY

TRANSLATED BY
KATE DEIMLING

AMAZON**CROSSING**

Previously published as *Une Fille Comme Elle* by Éditions Robert Laffont/Versilio in France in 2018. Translated from French by Kate Deimling. First published in English by Amazon Crossing in 2020.

All illustrations used by permission from the artist Pauline Lévêque.

Published by Amazon Crossing, Seattle
www.apub.com

Amazon, the Amazon logo, and Amazon Crossing are trademarks of Amazon.com, Inc., or its affiliates.

ISBN-13: 9781542020541
ISBN-10: 1542020549

Cover design by Kimberly Glyder

Printed in the United States of America

To you, my longtime partner
To my children, who amaze me every moment

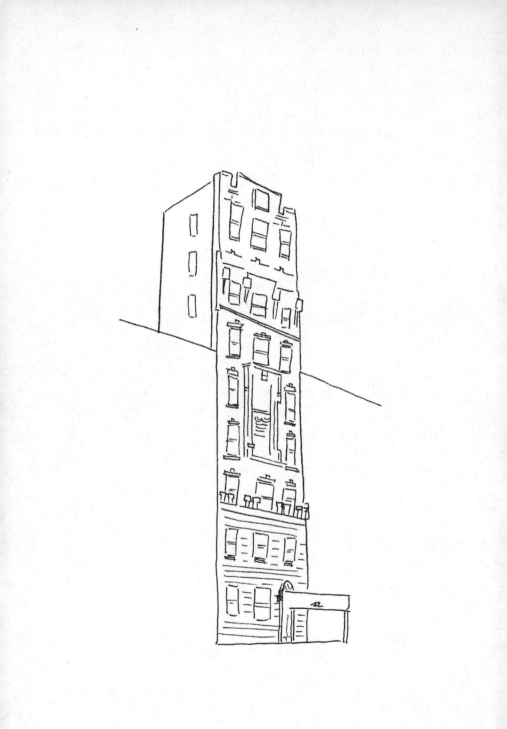

MY JOURNAL

The Day My Watch Stopped

First there was that smell, like fireworks, and the black night that returns when the colors of the grand finale disappear.

I remember opening my eyes and seeing my father's face full of anger and tears. Then my parents together, side by side—such an unlikely image that I thought it must have been a trick of the morphine.

The nurse took my blood pressure. At times when I'm falling asleep at night, I see her face again. I've been complimented on my smile—my friends say it gives me a certain charm—but Maggie's smile is beyond compare. People who meet her outside the hospital see only her largeness, but those who know her adore her for the size of her heart. I'll never understand why people only see thin as beautiful.

Julius was leaning against the door. The serious look on his face frightened me, and when he realized this, his features softened. I would have liked to make a joke, to find something clever to say to make all of them relax.

I could have asked them if I had won the race. I'm sure Dad would have laughed—well, maybe not. But no sound came out of my mouth. Then I was truly scared. Maggie gently explained that I had a tube in my throat and shouldn't try to speak or even swallow. Now that I was awake, they would take it out. I didn't feel at all like making my father laugh anymore.

Chloe

1

By the time rush hour begins in the late afternoon, Deepak has already
made three trips. A round trip to take Mr. Williams, a Fox News commentator, to the eighth floor. Another one to bring Mr. Groomlat, the
accountant, to his office on the second floor. And now, a trip to the
seventh floor with the golden retriever belonging to the Clercs, a French
couple. Their housekeeper comes to collect the dog on the landing and
give Deepak a ten-dollar bill, which he immediately brings to the dog
walker awaiting payment in the lobby.

Deepak looks at his watch. Mrs. Collins will be calling him soon.
The widow keeps her door locked with a dead bolt and chain, as if
anyone could get into the building without encountering Deepak first.
But the obsessions of the residents of 12 5th Avenue are part of his daily
routine. In fact, they *are* his routine.

After helping Mrs. Collins get her key out of the lock, he takes her
to the ground floor and then returns right away to the second floor.
Miss Chloe is waiting for him in front of the elevator and greets him
with a smile. She must have been born with a smile on her face. As she
enters the elevator, she asks him how his day has been.

"It's had its ups and downs, Miss Chloe."

Bringing the elevator to a stop exactly in line with each floor requires true skill. Deepak can do it with his eyes closed, but when he takes Chloe from her office on the second floor to her apartment on the ninth, he is especially careful.

"Will you be going out this evening?" he asks.

He's not trying to pry. Deepak simply needs to know if he should inform his nighttime counterpart that Chloe will require his services.

"No, just a hot bath and off to bed. Is my dad home?"

"You'll see soon enough."

Deepak practices two religions: Hinduism and discretion. Throughout his thirty-nine years as an elevator operator in this posh 5th Avenue apartment building, he has never revealed the slightest bit of information regarding the comings and goings of his employers. Especially not to their relatives.

◆ ◆ ◆

Twelve 5th Avenue is a stone-façade building with one apartment on each of its nine stories, except for the second, where there are two offices. With an average of five round trips per floor per day, factoring in the height of the ceilings, Deepak travels 594 kilometers per year. Since the beginning of his career, he has covered 23,166. He once calculated the figures in feet and miles but found the result too imprecise for his purposes. Like an aviator logging his flight hours, Deepak tucks a little notebook in the inside pocket of his uniform jacket where he keeps track of his vertical journeys.

In five months and three weeks, he will have traveled 23,448 kilometers, which is exactly three thousand times the elevation of Nanda Devi, the tallest mountain located entirely within India's borders. He has dreamed of climbing Nanda Devi, the Bliss-Giving Goddess, his whole life. His goal? To set the world record for most miles traveled vertically.

Deepak's manually operated elevator is an ancient artifact. There are only fifty-three such elevators left in all of New York. But for those who live in this apartment building, it is a reminder of a way of life.

Deepak is the master of a dying art. He isn't sure if he should be proud or saddened by this.

Every morning at 6:15, Deepak enters 12 5th Avenue by the service entrance. He goes downstairs to the basement and heads to his locker in the storeroom. He hangs up his baggy pants and unfashionable sweater and puts on a white shirt, flannel pants, and a uniform coat with the building's address embroidered on the front in gold letters. He smooths back his fine hair and places a cap on his head. Then he takes a look at himself in the little mirror attached to the storeroom door and heads up to relieve Mr. Rivera.

For the next half hour, he cleans the inside of the elevator: first the woodwork with a soft cloth and polish, and then the copper handle. Climbing aboard his elevator is like taking a short trip on the Orient Express, or, if you look up to admire the Renaissance fresco on the ceiling, ascending to heaven in a royal chariot.

A modern elevator would be much more affordable for the apartment owners. But how can you put a price on a friendly hello and an attentive ear? How can you attach monetary value to someone who patiently and diplomatically resolves disputes between neighbors, brightens your morning with a cheerful word or two, informs you about the weather, wishes you a happy birthday, watches over your apartment when you're out of town, and reassures you with his presence when you come home in anticipation of a long and lonely night? Being an elevator operator is not just a job: it's sacred work.

For thirty-nine years, all Deepak's days have been alike. Between the morning and evening rush hours, he settles in at his desk in the lobby. He takes any visitors up in the elevator, after first locking the front door. He also receives packages and cleans the large mirror in the lobby and the glass of the wrought-iron doors twice a day. At 6:15 p.m., Deepak hands over his kingdom to Mr. Rivera. He goes back down to the basement, hangs up his white shirt, flannel pants, and uniform coat, places his cap on a shelf, changes into his street clothes, smooths back his hair, takes a look at himself in the mirror, and heads to the subway.

Deepak usually gets a seat on the train he catches at the West 4th Street–Washington Square station, a seat he always gives to the first female passenger who enters when the train fills up at 34th Street. When it empties out at 42nd, Deepak sits down again, opens his newspaper, and reads about world events until he gets off the subway at 116th Street. Then he walks the ten blocks to his building. He makes this trip morning and night, in the hot summer sun, in the autumn rain, and with snowstorms raging in the wintry skies.

At 7:30, he has dinner with his wife at home. Lali and Deepak have deviated from this routine only once in thirty-nine years. Lali was twenty-six at the time, and Deepak feverishly held her hand in the ambulance as the contractions started coming faster and faster. What should have been the most wonderful day of their lives turned into a tragedy that was never spoken of again.

Every other Thursday, Lali and Deepak have a romantic dinner together in a little restaurant in Spanish Harlem.

Deepak is fond of his orderly life and devoted to his wife.

As he sits down to dinner this particular night, he has no idea that his life is about to be turned upside down.

2

The Air India flight landed on the tarmac at JFK. Sanji got up, grabbed his bag from the overhead compartment, and rushed to the Jetway, thrilled to be the first one off the plane. He strode quickly through the airport and, a bit out of breath, entered the large space where the immigration officers were lined up in their booths. An unfriendly officer questioned him about his reasons for visiting New York. Sanji answered that he was on a research trip and showed him the letter from his aunt vouching for his ability to support himself. The officer ignored Sanji's letter, gave a cursory glance at the visa in his passport, and then lifted his head to examine Sanji. For Sanji, like any foreigner, a moment of uncertainty ensued. Would he be singled out for his appearance, led into an interrogation room, and sent back home for any number of reasons? The officer finally stamped his passport, scribbled the date by which he had to leave the United States, and told him to move along.

Sanji picked up his suitcase from the carousel, passed through customs, and walked to the area where limousine drivers were waiting. He spotted his name on a sign. The driver relieved him of his luggage and escorted him to the car.

The black limo moved along the Long Island Expressway, weaving through the swiftly flowing traffic as night fell. The seat was soft, and Sanji, tired from the trip, felt like drifting off to sleep. The driver made this impossible by starting up a conversation as the skyscrapers of Manhattan materialized in the distance.

"Business or pleasure?"

"Why not both?" Sanji answered.

"Bridge or tunnel?"

"Sorry?"

"This is a limo, not a helicopter, so you have to choose one or the other."

"I'm not sure I—"

"Forget it, I'm gonna take the Queensboro Bridge, there's a great view. You from India?"

"Mumbai."

"Maybe you'll end up driving, like me, that's what most Indians do when they get here. Most drive yellow cabs, some drive for Uber, and a select few drive limousines like this one."

Sanji looked at the medallion displayed in the car. The driver's photo appeared alongside his name, Marius Zobonya, and his license number, 8451.

"Are there any Polish doctors, teachers, or engineers in New York?"

Marius scratched his chin.

"Not that I know of. But my wife's physical therapist is Slovakian."

"That's good to hear. I hate driving."

The driver left it at that. Sanji took out his cell phone and checked his messages. His time in New York was going to be very busy. He should probably get the family visit out of the way as soon as possible. In keeping with tradition, he needed to thank his aunt, who had so kindly written him a letter of reference. It had been especially kind, as he had never met her.

"How far are we from Harlem?" he asked.

"Harlem's big. East or West?"

Sanji unfolded the letter and checked the address on the back of the envelope.

"225 East 118th Street."

"Fifteen minutes, tops."

"Great, take me there. I'll go to the Plaza afterward."

The car headed up the FDR Drive along the East River and then the Harlem River and stopped in front of a seventies-era redbrick apartment building.

"Are you sure this is it?" asked Marius.

"Yes, why?"

"Because this is a Puerto Rican neighborhood."

"Maybe my aunt is a Puerto Rican Indian," Sanji said drily.

"Want me to wait?"

"Yes, it won't take long."

Just to be safe, he took his suitcase from the trunk and walked toward the building.

◆ ◆ ◆

When Lali lifted the lid of the casserole dish, the aroma wafted through the dining room. Upon returning home, Deepak had been surprised to see her in a sari (she never wore one), but the fact that she had prepared his favorite dish surprised him even more. She only made it on holidays. Maybe his wife was finally coming to her senses. Why treat yourself only on special occasions? After the food was served, Deepak caught her up on the news of the day. He liked to give a detailed summary of what he had read on the subway. Lali listened to him distractedly.

"I may have forgotten to tell you that I had a call from Mumbai," she mentioned while serving him seconds.

"From Mumbai?" Deepak repeated.

"Yes, from our nephew."

"Which one? We must have twenty nephews and nieces, and we don't know any of them."

"My brother's son."

"Oh." Deepak yawned, feeling himself getting sleepy. "How's he doing?"

"My brother's been dead for twenty years."

"Not him, your nephew!"

"You'll see soon enough."

Deepak put down his fork.

"What exactly do you mean by 'soon enough'?"

"Well, the line was bad," Lali said with a shrug. "But I think he said he wanted to come to New York and needed a place to stay."

"What does that have to do with us?"

"Deepak, ever since we left Mumbai, you've gone on about the splendors of India—but it's always felt as far away as a fairy tale. And now India is coming to you, and you're going to complain?"

"It's not India coming to me but your nephew. What do you know about him? Is he a respectable person? If he's coming to us for a place to stay, he must be broke."

"We were broke when we moved here."

"But we were determined to work. We didn't camp out with strangers."

"A few weeks isn't the end of the world."

"At my age, a few weeks might be all I have left!"

"Don't be so melodramatic. In any case, you're not even here during the day. I'm looking forward to showing him the city. You're not going to deprive me of that pleasure, are you?"

"Where will he sleep?"

Lali glanced down the hallway.

"Out of the question!"

Deepak put down his napkin, walked across the living room, and opened the door to the blue room. He had painted it that color three decades earlier. Taking apart the crib he had made with his own hands had been the most painful experience of his life. Ever since, he entered that room only once a year, to sit down in the chair he had placed near the window and offer a silent prayer.

When Deepak saw how his wife had transformed the room, he was at a loss for words.

Lali put her arms around him from behind.

"A bit of youthful energy could do us some good."

"So when does this nephew of yours arrive?" asked Deepak as the intercom buzzed.

❖ ❖ ❖

Waiting for her guest in the doorway of the apartment, Lali adjusted her sari and ran her hand over her hair, which she wore in a bun secured with an ivory comb.

The elevator door opened, and Sanji stepped out wearing jeans, a white shirt, a tailor-made jacket, and stylish sneakers.

"You don't look the way I imagined," Lali said, a little embarrassed. "Please make yourself at home."

"We'll see about that," grumbled Deepak from behind her. "I'll make some tea for our passing guest while you go change."

"Don't listen to this grumpy old man," she cut in. "Deepak is making fun of my outfit. I didn't know what kind of man would knock at our door. Our family was always so conservative."

"India has changed a lot. You were expecting me?"

"Of course I was expecting you." Lali sighed, gazing at him. "You look so much like him. It's like seeing my brother again after forty years."

"Don't bother him with those old stories, he must be exhausted," Deepak said, leading the guest to the dining room.

When Lali came back after swapping her sari for pants and a blouse, she found the two men seated at the table making polite conversation with noticeable effort. She put out some cookies, asked her nephew if he'd had a good flight, and listed all the places that she wanted to show him. Lali tried to make up for her husband's quietness. Sanji waited for the moment when he could leave without being rude. He stifled a yawn, which gave Deepak an opening: it was high time everyone went to bed.

"Your room is ready," Lali announced.

"My room?" repeated Sanji.

She took her nephew by the hand and led him to the blue room. Sanji studied it warily.

On the corduroy-covered sofa bed, Lali had spread out orange sheets and placed two flowered pillows and a handmade patchwork quilt. She had also commandeered the table from the entrance to use as a makeshift desk and adorned it with a terra-cotta pot full of paper flowers.

"I hope you like it. I'm so happy to have you stay with us."

She closed the curtains and said good night.

Sanji looked at his watch. It was 8:15. The idea of sacrificing a junior suite at the Plaza with a view of Central Park for an eight-by-eight room in Spanish Harlem horrified him, and he wondered how he could extricate himself from this sticky situation without offending his aunt. Finally, a prisoner of propriety and with a lump in his throat, he called the limo driver to say that he no longer needed his services. As he heard the sofa bed creak beneath him, his thoughts turned to the king-size bed that should have been his.

◆ ◆ ◆

At 12 5th Avenue, Chloe opened the door to her 2,700-square-foot apartment. She put her keys on the entryway table and gazed at the photos in the hallway as she passed. The walls were practically a gallery of her life. She liked some of the pictures, such as the one of her father at age thirty, with his thick hair and his Indiana Jones look that used to drive her high school girlfriends crazy. But she hated the one where she was receiving a medal after a race in San Francisco, because her mother looked so sour-faced. (She would pack her bags and leave the next day.) And she felt nostalgic about the picture of the dog who was once part of the family, back when she and her parents were still together.

A ray of light came from the office. She entered silently and watched her father. His once-red hair was as thick as ever, but its color had turned to ash. Bent over his desk, Professor Bronstein was grading papers.

"Did you have a good day?" she asked.

"Teaching Keynesian economics to a bunch of zit-faced kids is more fun than it sounds. How was your audition?" he asked without looking up.

"I'll find out in a few days if I get a callback."

"Aren't you having dinner with Schopenhauer?"

Chloe looked at her father and moved back toward the door.

"Would you like to go out to dinner, the two of us? I can be ready in half an hour," she said as she left.

"Twenty minutes!" he called after her.

"That's how long it takes just to fill the bathtub. I'll be on your schedule if you ever get the plumbing fixed!" he heard from afar.

Professor Bronstein opened a drawer and dug through his papers until he found an old repair estimate. He sat back in dismay when he read the amount. He put it back and immersed himself in grading papers until Chloe knocked on his door decidedly more than half an hour later.

"I called Mr. Rivera, let's go."

Mr. Bronstein put his jacket on and joined his daughter on the landing. The elevator gate was already open. Chloe entered first, and her father followed.

"Deepak said you weren't going out tonight," the elevator operator said almost apologetically.

"Change of plans!" Chloe said cheerfully.

Rivera turned the handle, and the elevator began to descend.

On the ground floor, he slid the gate open and moved out of the way to let Chloe go by.

Outside, the sky was midnight blue, the temperature mild.

"Let's go to Claudette's," suggested the professor.

"We can't take advantage of their generosity forever. Someday we'll have to pay our tab."

"Not forever, but we can do it a little bit longer. You should be happy—I finally paid the grocer today."

"How about Mimi's? My treat."

"Did you hit your mother up for money?" Mr. Bronstein asked in a worried voice.

"Not exactly. I did go visit her. We were supposed to spend some time together, but she was busy packing. Her gigolo is taking her to Mexico. Well, actually, she's taking him. So, to make herself feel better, she handed me some cash and told me to go buy some new clothes."

"Maybe you should have."

"She hates my taste in clothes. Whereas you and I share the same taste for French cuisine," she said, heading down the street.

"Not so fast, I'm on foot, you know!" Mr. Bronstein protested. "And stop calling Rodrigo that, they've been living together for fifteen years."

"He's twenty years younger than she is, and he lives off her income."

Passing Washington Square Park, they turned down Sullivan Street. Inside the entrance of Mimi's, the hostess welcomed them, loudly announcing that their table was ready, even though ten customers were sitting at the bar waiting to be seated. As regulars, they were entitled to certain privileges. The professor slid into the booth while the waiter removed the chair across from him to make room for Chloe's wheelchair. She turned toward a couple who had not stopped staring at them.

"It's a Karman S-115, a limited edition. I highly recommend it, it's very comfortable and easy to fold," she said before turning to join her father.

"I'm having the gnocchi à la Parisienne, what about you?" he asked tensely.

Chloe chose the French onion soup and ordered two glasses of Pomerol.

"So who stood up whom?" asked Mr. Bronstein.

"What are you talking about?"

"This morning, you said you'd be back late, and I heard you rummaging around in your closet for quite a while."

"I was going to go out with the girls, but after the audition, I was so tired that—"

"Chloe, please!"

"Julius is really busy, so I suggested we do it another night."

"Being a philosophy professor with the name Schopenhauer is a real cross to bear, I'm sure."

"Could we please change the subject?"

"Whatever happened to that patient of yours? As I recall, her boyfriend took her for granted. You said his behavior made her unhappy, but also, paradoxically, made her happy at the same time."

"That isn't exactly what I said. It's kind of like Stockholm syndrome. She thinks she's so worthless that she feels grateful for the love he gives her."

"Didn't you tell her to leave him for someone better?"

"My job is simply to listen to my patients and help them become aware of what they're expressing."

"Did you find a solution to her problem, at least?"

"Well, I'm working on it—I'm teaching her to expect more, and she's making a lot of progress. But if you're trying to tell me something, please just come out and say it."

"Just that you should expect as much as any other woman."

"That's your way of changing the subject? I think you have over-protective-father syndrome."

"Maybe you're right. If only I could have consulted you before your mother left me . . . but you were only thirteen," the professor said with a sigh. "Why do you run around from one audition to the next when you're so good at what you do?"

"Because I'm just starting out as a therapist. I only have three patients, and we have no money."

"It's not up to you to support us. If all goes well, I'm about to clinch a lecture series that will get our finances back in shape."

"But you'll be away all the time and you'll be exhausted. It's time for me to be independent again."

"We should move. That apartment is too expensive for us."

"No way. I put my life back together again in that apartment twice, once when we left Connecticut and again after my accident, and besides, I want you to be able to grow old there."

"I'm afraid I'm already old."

"You're only fifty-seven, and those people watching us think we're a couple."

"What people?"

"At the table behind me."

"How do you know they're looking at us?"

"I can just tell."

Chloe and her father often ended their evenings out with a private game. They looked at each other without speaking, and each had to guess what the other was thinking through facial expressions and head movements alone. The people around them always noticed these subtle exchanges. It was one of the few times Chloe liked being watched, when she knew people were looking at her instead of her wheelchair.

3

The floral organza curtains barely blocked the morning light, which awakened Sanji at dawn. For a moment, he didn't know where he was, but then he was reminded by the pink and blue of the room. He buried his head under the pillow and went back to sleep. He woke suddenly a few hours later, grabbed his cell phone from the nightstand, and jumped out of bed. He dressed hastily and left the room, his hair sticking up all over.

Lali was waiting for him at the kitchen table.

"So, do you want to go to the Met or the Guggenheim? Or maybe you'd like to walk around Chinatown, Little Italy, Nolita, or Soho? We can go anywhere you like."

"Where's the bathroom?" he asked in a daze.

Lali pointed down the hall, obviously disappointed.

Sanji returned a few minutes later, his hair combed.

"Have some breakfast," Lali ordered.

Sanji sat down on the chair that Lali had pushed back with her foot.

"Okay," he agreed. "But something quick, I'm running late."

"What kind of work do you do, if I may ask?" she asked as she poured milk into a bowl of cereal.

"I work in the tech world."

"What does that mean, exactly?"

"We design new technologies that make people's lives easier."

"Could you design a nephew for me who would spice up my routine? Someone I could go for a walk with, someone who would tell me about my country or give me news of my family, whom I haven't been in touch with for so long?"

Sanji got up and kissed his aunt on the forehead.

"I promise," he said, embarrassed by his own spontaneous show of emotion. "As soon as I can, but I really have to go to work now."

"Okay, get going, I'm already getting too used to you being here. And just so you know, it's out of the question for you to stay anywhere except under my roof while you're in New York. I'd be extremely annoyed. You wouldn't dream of offending a member of your family, would you?"

With no other choice but to leave his suitcase behind, Sanji left the apartment.

It was a beautiful spring day to see Spanish Harlem for the first time. He took in the colorful store windows, crowded sidewalks, and packed streets with car horns blasting. The only things missing from this mayhem were the rickshaws. A twenty-hour flight just to be teleported into a Puerto Rican version of Mumbai! Before going down into the subway, he sealed his fate by calling the Plaza to cancel his reservation.

Since his aunt had left, India had modernized in many ways. But some traditions stuck—respecting your elders was still nonnegotiable.

Sanji got off the subway at West 4th Street, already late for his meeting. As he walked along the iron fence of Washington Square Park, he heard a melody. Instead of going around the park, he crossed through it, like a child following the Pied Piper, and came upon a musician playing the trumpet. The notes rose up among the branches of the linden and catalpa trees, the Norway maples, the Chinese elms. Twenty or so people had gathered around the performer. Sanji came closer and sat down on a bench, completely under the music's spell.

"This will be our song. You'd better not forget it," a young woman whispered nearby.

Surprised, he turned his head.

"There's always some melody when two people meet," she added playfully.

She was radiant.

"I'm joking. You looked so mesmerized—it was very sweet."

"My father was a wonderful clarinet player. 'Petite Fleur' was his favorite song—he played it all the time when I was little."

"Feeling homesick?"

"I'm all right, I haven't been here very long."

"Did you travel far?"

"From Spanish Harlem, just a half hour away."

"Touché—we're even," she replied with a smile.

"I'm from Mumbai. And you?"

"I live on that corner."

"Do you come here often?"

"Almost every morning."

"Maybe we'll see each other again. I've got to run."

"Do you have a name?"

"Yes."

"Nice to meet you, Yes. I'm Chloe."

Sanji smiled and waved, and went on his way.

The building where Sam worked was on the corner of West 4th Street and MacDougal, along the southern side of the park. Sanji went up to the desk, and the receptionist asked him to wait a moment.

"You haven't changed at all," Sanji exclaimed upon seeing his friend.

"Neither have you, just as punctual as always. They don't do wake-up calls at the Plaza?"

"I'm staying somewhere else," Sanji answered nonchalantly. "Let's get to work!"

Sam and Sanji had met fifteen years earlier at Oxford. Sanji was studying computer science; and Sam, economics. England had seemed more foreign to Sam, an American, than it had to Sanji.

When he returned to India, Sanji founded a successful company. Sam moved to New York and worked as an account manager at an investment firm.

Their friendship continued over e-mail, and they were in touch regularly, so when Sanji got the idea of raising money in the United States to expand his company, he called on Sam. Sanji hated talking about money, which was somewhat inconvenient for an entrepreneur.

The morning was devoted to developing the materials they would give to potential investors. The numbers projected were tantalizing, but Sam thought Sanji's presentation was unclear, and he kept interrupting him.

"You're way too vague and off topic. The investors have to see you as a long-term partner, not just an app designer, however brilliant. They're fantasizing about India."

"What, do you want me to wear a turban and roll my r's to seem more exotic?"

"It would be more stylish than jeans and a wrinkled shirt. America is full of software developers. Your social network has hundreds of thousands of users in Mumbai alone—that's what the investors will be excited about."

"Maybe you should do the presentation. You seem to know what to say and what not to say better than I do."

Sam studied his friend. Sanji was from a wealthy Indian family. Sam's parents owned a hardware store in Wisconsin, and he had gotten through school on scholarships and loans that he had only recently paid off.

Pulling off this deal would prove to his boss that he could handle big projects, and he might even be made a partner.

Sam was pragmatic, and he wasn't jealous of Sanji—in fact, he admired him. But he fully intended to use Sanji's family's reputation to attract his clients, even if his friend had noble reasons for not wanting to rely on it.

"Sure, why not? In college, I always got better grades than you on oral exams," Sam said.

"If classes had been in Hindi, things would have been different."

"Who knows? Go take a walk. When you get back, I'll do the presentation for you, and you can see if I'm more convincing than you are!"

"When should I be back for this marvelous performance?"

"An hour, tops."

Leaving the building, Sanji found himself walking alongside the park. The trumpet player had gone, and with it the melody. He called his aunt and asked her to lunch.

◆ ◆ ◆

Lali met him in front of the fountain in Washington Square Park.

"I feel like having a gourmet meal. Pick the best restaurant in the neighborhood, and it's my treat," Sanji said upon seeing his aunt.

"No need to waste your money—I brought us a basketful of goodies."

As she spread out a tablecloth on the grass and took out paper plates and plastic utensils, Sanji wondered if fate was conspiring against him.

"It's funny that we're meeting in this park," said Lali.

"Why? My partner's office is close by."

"Well, my partner also works close by." Lali continued unpacking the basket.

21

"What was my father like as a child?"

"He was reserved, always observing other people. Kind of like you. Don't deny it—last night, you hardly took your eyes off Deepak. But I doubt you saw much, because behind that grumpy face hides a man who's full of surprises. In fact, he's never stopped surprising me."

"What does he do for a living?"

"What is this, a police interrogation? You haven't told me anything about yourself."

"Does he drive a taxi?"

"An elevator," said Lali with a smile. "He has spent his life in a tiny compartment that's even older than he is."

"How did you meet?"

"We met at Shivaji Park. I loved going to the cricket matches. I went there every Sunday. It was my taste of freedom. If my father had known that I was watching boys play sports, I would have been in hot water. Deepak was a great batsman. He finally noticed me sitting alone in the bleachers. I was quite pretty when I was young. One day, during a close game, Deepak looked over at me and missed the ball, and everyone was surprised, because normally the other teams' bowlers could never get him out. But I wasn't surprised. When the match was over, he came and sat two rows below me, just in case anyone saw us. He said that he had been seriously humiliated because of me, and that to make it up to him, I had to agree to see him again. Which I did the next Sunday, but this time we left the park and walked along Mahim Bay. We sat down near a temple that looks out on the pier. We started talking, and we've never stopped. We've been together for almost forty years, and when he leaves in the morning, I miss him. Sometimes I even come to this park and walk around, just to be near him. He works on 5th Avenue, at number twelve," she said, pointing toward the Washington Square Arch. "But he hates it if I go and bother him. That damn building is his personal kingdom."

Lali stopped speaking and gazed at her nephew.

"I see myself in your eyes, not my brother."

"What do you see, then?" Sanji asked skeptically.

"Pride and dreams."

"I have to get back to work."

"Back to the tech world?"

"It's my own personal kingdom. I have dinner plans, so don't wait up. I'll be quiet when I come in."

"I'll hear you anyway. Have fun, and tomorrow, or some other day, we'll go visit some of my favorite places."

Sanji walked his aunt to the subway station. As he headed back to Sam's office, his eyes wandered to the awning of 12 5th Avenue.

◆ ◆ ◆

A building's lobby holds its history. It's the backdrop to its residents' stories, the people who live side by side but often barely know each other. The milestones of their lives are ushered through the stairwells—births, marriages, divorces, and deaths—but their daily privacy is protected behind the fine apartments' thick walls.

The lobby Sanji entered was paneled with oak. The elegant décor was illuminated by a large chandelier and crystal sconces, and the center of the gleaming marble floor was inlaid with a black granite rosette and a star pointing in the four cardinal directions. The building's original charm had been painstakingly preserved. On the reception desk sat an antiquated Bakelite telephone. Once it had been used to call the doorman, but it had been silent for ages. A black notebook whose pages were slowly filled with visitors' names was open on the desk. And behind it, Deepak was dozing. The click of the front door had not roused him.

Sanji cleared his throat, and Deepak awoke with a start.

"How may I help you?" he asked politely, adjusting his glasses.

Seeing Sanji, he frowned.

"What are you doing here?"

"I came to see this place that my aunt described in such glowing terms."

"Haven't you ever seen an apartment building? Do you live in the Dharavi slum?"

"I wanted to see the famous elevator—"

"Lali told you about that, too, did she?"

"Apparently it's beautiful and you have to be an expert to operate it."

"That's true," he said, flattered.

Deepak turned around to make sure they were alone. He grabbed his cap and put it on his head. In this fine uniform, Sanji thought his uncle looked like the captain of a ship.

"All right," he grumbled. "No one is going to call for a while, so follow me and I'll give you a tour. But be quiet, okay?"

Sanji agreed. He felt as if he had been given permission to visit a museum after hours. Deepak slid open the gate of the elevator and beckoned for his nephew to enter. With his hand on the handle, he waited for a few moments, as if to give a more solemn feeling to the short trip they were about to take.

"Listen closely," he said. "Every sound is important."

Sanji heard an electric crackling and the hum of the motor as it came to life. The elevator slowly rose with a whoosh of air.

"You see, it plays music, with a different note at every floor. I can recognize the notes with my eyes closed. They let me know where I am and exactly when I need to lower this handle to gently stop the elevator."

The elevator came to a stop right at the level of the sixth floor. Deepak stood still, waiting for a show of appreciation with such an expectant look on his face that Sanji did his best to look impressed.

"Going down is even better and requires a lot of skill, because of the counterweight, which is heavier than we are. Do you understand?"

Sanji nodded. As the elevator started to move, Deepak's cell phone rang. He turned the handle, stopping the elevator.

"Is it broken?" asked Sanji.

"Be quiet, I'm thinking. I'm needed on the ninth floor," he said, turning the handle once more.

The elevator ascended, much faster than before.

"You can even adjust the speed?"

"It must be Mr. Bronstein, but this isn't his usual time. Stay behind me and don't say a word. If he says hello, say hello back, as if you're just visiting someone."

A young woman in a wheelchair was waiting on the landing, facing away from them in order to enter backward.

"Good morning, miss," Deepak said politely.

"Yes, good morning again, Deepak . . ."

Sanji scooted back against the wall to make room for her.

"Aren't you going to stop and drop this gentleman off somewhere?" asked Chloe as they passed the second floor.

Deepak didn't need to explain since the elevator had now settled onto the ground floor. He slid the gate open and just barely managed to stop Sanji from trying to help Chloe. Deepak rushed out into the lobby to open the door for her.

"Do you need a taxi?"

"Yes, please," she answered.

And then several things happened at once. Someone showed up to deliver a package while the bell behind the desk rang three times. Deepak asked the deliveryman to wait for a moment, which didn't seem to make him happy.

"Three rings is Mr. Morrison," Deepak muttered. "But let me get your taxi first."

"Who's gonna sign for this package?" asked the deliveryman, following them outside.

Chloe grabbed it, put it on her lap, and signed the slip.

"Ooh, it's for the Clercs. I wonder what it is?" she asked conspiratorially.

Deepak shot a meaningful look at his nephew, who was waiting under the awning. Sanji stepped over to Chloe and took the package.

"I'll leave it on the desk, unless you want to open it first," he said.

He came right back. Deepak was in the middle of the avenue, with his whistle at his lips. But he let three yellow cabs with their lights on pass by without trying to flag them down.

"I don't want to stick my nose where it doesn't belong, but the bell is still ringing," Sanji informed him.

"Deepak, go and get Mr. Morrison, I can manage on my own," Chloe said.

"I'll get a taxi," Sanji suggested, coming closer to his uncle.

"Not just any taxi, only the minivans that are handicapped accessible," whispered Deepak.

"Of course! I don't know who this Mr. Morrison is, but he doesn't seem very patient."

In a bind, Deepak hesitated, and then dashed into the building, leaving Sanji with Chloe.

"Is everything okay?" he asked.

"Why wouldn't everything be okay?" she replied curtly.

"No reason, I just thought I heard you say something."

"I should have left earlier. I'm going to be late."

"For something important?"

"Yes, very important . . . at least I hope so."

He dashed out into the street and stopped a taxi. A regular one.

Chloe approached him. "It's very nice of you to almost get run over, and I don't want to seem ungrateful, but I'm going to have a hard time getting into this one."

"You're late, aren't you?"

Without waiting for an answer, Sanji leaned over, picked her up in his arms, and gently placed her on the back seat. Then he folded up the wheelchair, put it in the trunk, and came back to shut the door.

"There you go!" he said, pleased with himself.

Chloe looked him in the eyes.

"Can I just ask you one little thing?"

"Sure," he replied, leaning over the door.

"How am I supposed to get out when I get there?"

Sanji looked baffled.

"When is your appointment?"

"In fifteen minutes, just enough time to make it there, if traffic isn't too bad."

Sanji looked at his watch, walked around the taxicab, and got in next to Chloe.

"Let's go," he said.

"Go where?" asked Chloe.

"Wherever your appointment is."

"Park Avenue and 28th Street."

"I'm going the same way," he said as the taxi pulled away.

Silence. Chloe looked out the window, and Sanji did the same.

"There's no reason to feel awkward about it," he said at last. "I'll just drop you off and—"

"Actually, I was thinking about the joke I made in the park a little while ago. I hope you didn't take it the wrong way. I'm sorry, I didn't expect us to run into each other again, especially not the very same day. What were you doing in my elevator?"

"Going up and down."

"Is that a hobby of yours?"

"What's this important appointment? If you don't mind me asking."

"An audition. What about you? What are you doing at 28th Street?"

"It's also an audition, but with investors."

"You're in finance?"

"Is it for TV or the movies?"

"I didn't know we had this in common."

"'We'?"

"I'm Jewish. An atheist, but still Jewish."

"And what do we have in common?"

"Answering a question with another question."

"So I can't be Indian and Jewish at the same time?"

"You just proved my point!"

The car pulled over to the curb.

"Right on time! I'll tell you what I do for a living if we happen to meet again," said Sanji as he got out.

He opened the trunk, unfolded the wheelchair, and helped Chloe into it.

"And why would we meet again?"

"Good luck with the audition," he said as he got back into the taxi.

She watched as it made a U-turn and headed back downtown.

◆ ◆ ◆

Sanji's cell phone hadn't stopped vibrating the whole cab ride. Sam must have been bouncing off the walls of his office.

Sanji arrived, with no explanation for his tardiness or the dreamy look on his face. Sam didn't even try to hide his irritation but jumped straight into his version of the presentation. Sanji observed his friend's performance, and, although he found it lacking in creative flair, he didn't have the nerve to say so under the circumstances.

They agreed that the next morning, Sam would present the project to one of his biggest clients and Sanji would simply grace them with his presence.

After dinner in Chinatown, Sam offered to drop Sanji off at his hotel.

"That's nice of you, but I'm staying in Spanish Harlem."

"What the hell are you doing in Spanish Harlem?" Sam exclaimed.

Sanji explained the situation and his aunt's misunderstanding.

"Why didn't you ask me to write the letter?"

"You were already doing a lot for me."

"You're insane! Giving up a suite at the Plaza with room service and breakfast in bed to go stay with strangers—either you're crazy or a masochist!"

"They're not strangers," said Sanji as he got into a taxi.

◆ ◆ ◆

The springs of the sofa bed were poking into Sanji's back. He got up and opened the curtains. The cheerful noises of Spanish Harlem brought him back once more to Mumbai. Sanji believed in signs, and he wondered about the series of circumstances that had led him to this little room overlooking a Puerto Rican bodega in the apartment of an aunt he had never met. All while he had been so determined to flee his family!

The break with his family had taken place after his father collapsed at the dinner table midsentence. His body wasn't even cold when his uncles had started arguing about the future of the Mumbai Palace Hotel. Sanji had promised himself he would never be like them. He had listened silently as they talked in code about the inheritance and the new division of roles in the company. He then slipped away for a moment of silent prayer beside the body of a man who had taught him so much but whom he hadn't spent a lot of time with.

According to his uncles, a mother could not raise a child alone—a son needed paternal authority. They decided to take the fatherless Sanji under their wing. From that moment on, Sanji swore he'd escape them.

Boarding schools and tutors made for an austere childhood. Sanji counted the days until school vacations, when he could finally see his mother again. He was later sent even farther away, to Oxford. The definitive break with his family occurred when he came back from England. Sanji happened to run into an old classmate. The conversation soon turned to women. It was generally understood that young people in India could spend time together as long as it wasn't serious. Deciding whom they would love was up to their families.

Sanji had an idea. Since their carefree youth would soon be taken away, why not find a way to enjoy it as much as possible right now? He had the idea of developing an app so that people could meet each other without relying on chance, an app that could extend their horizons beyond the circle of family or professional connections. The social network he imagined would be much more sophisticated than the ones developed in America. The first versions of his program quickly attracted several thousand users, and their numbers kept growing. He needed more capital to improve the interface, hire employees, rent offices, and market the app to attract even more users. Sanji had inherited his father's fortune, although most of it was in the form of shares in the Mumbai Palace Hotel, of which he owned a third. His success surpassed his wildest dreams. One year after its launch, the platform was up to one hundred thousand users. Now it had almost reached one million.

The *Daily News* had covered his success, but one journalist raised an issue that haunted Indian society: Would the social network Sanji had created radically change the culture, and how far should it be allowed to go? The article got a lot of attention, and it sowed much discord between Sanji and his uncles. Only his mother was still on his side, even though she didn't understand much about what her son was doing. He was happy, and that was all that mattered to her.

One day, while visiting his sick mother, Sanji sat at her bedside flipping through family photo albums. He noticed a face he didn't recognize. He learned from his mother that the young woman in the photo was his father's sister. An aunt whom he had never met because she had abandoned her family to marry some good-for-nothing and run off to America.

When his mother recovered, Sanji plunged himself back into his work. He needed new capital to grow. Indian banks were reluctant to get involved because his company was constantly being lambasted by the conservative press. Then Sanji had the idea of drumming up investors where his competitors had prospered—America. It had taken just a visa and a letter to an aunt he'd never met to get him here, to this awful sofa bed.

Sanji closed the curtains again, wondering what the next sign would be.

"Can't sleep?" Lali asked, opening the door to his room. "I'm an insomniac, too. I don't know if it's a curse or a blessing—the less you sleep, the more you live, right?"

"That's not what the doctors say."

"Are you hungry? Want me to heat something up for you? We don't have to worry about waking Deepak, he'd sleep through an earthquake."

Sanji sat down at the kitchen table. Lali got out the *badam halwa* and dished out two large portions of the almond-flavored Indian dessert.

"So, which is it? Insomnia or jet lag?"

"Neither. I was just thinking."

"Are you worried? Do you need money?" Lali asked.

"No, what makes you think I need money?"

"I know your uncles. When my father died, they cheated me out of my share of the inheritance. Oh, I know the dilapidated apartments he owned weren't worth much, but it's the principle of the thing, you know," she added, taking her wallet out of her purse.

"You can put that away, I'm doing just fine on my own."

"No one does anything great all alone. Those who think so are full of themselves."

"Your husband is all alone in his elevator."

"Not quite. He works closely with a colleague who takes the night shift. And he has me. I've agreed to all his crazy ideas, even the ones that made no sense, I've let him have all the freedom he needed, but I've always insisted that he sleep next to me."

"Did you really leave India to be together?"

"I don't know how it is today, but in my day, marriages were arranged, and young people had no say in the matter. But I was never the type to let others decide for me. Deepak was from a different caste, but we loved each other and we were determined to decide our own future. We didn't realize that would mean leaving Mumbai before Deepak got himself killed by your grandfather or one of your uncles."

"My father would never have let something like that happen!"

"He took the men's side. I felt terribly betrayed. Of my three brothers, your father was the only one who understood me. He should have taken my side and stood up to our family's backward, hypocritical ways, but he didn't do it. But I shouldn't speak about him to you this way, it's not right."

It was very late. Sanji and Lali said good night, but sleep eluded both of them.

At 12 5th Avenue, everyone had been asleep for some time, except Mrs. Collins, whose alarm clock had just gone off. The charming older woman who lived in the apartment on the sixth floor put on her dressing gown and went into the living room. She covered her parrot's cage with a black silk scarf and entered the kitchen. She unbolted the service door and left it ajar. Next, she went into her bathroom, applied blush to her cheeks in front of the mirror, sprayed a little perfume on her neck, and slipped back into bed. She leafed through a magazine, waiting.

The Day I Left
the Hospital

In the beginning, I used a wooden board, placing it between the bed and the seat of the wheelchair and sliding across it. Maggie taught me this trick. She'd seen it all before, and she had a way of explaining things that didn't leave you any room to be afraid. She had promised me that if I built up my arms, one day I wouldn't need the board anymore. All those years of running to develop legs of steel—now that they weren't there anymore, I had to start from scratch with my arms and shoulders.

One morning, Dr. Mulder told me there was no need to keep me in the hospital any longer. He seemed sad as he said this, and I wondered if maybe he wanted me to stay. Since I had a bit of a thing for him, and Maggie had slipped me one last painkiller, I suggested we run away together. He laughed and patted my shoulder and said he was proud of me. Then he asked me to get ready, since apparently there were people waiting for me outside. What people? I asked. You'll see, he replied with a little smile that made me melt.

I didn't know what was going on, but at that moment, I had only one idea in my head: to preserve his face and his scent in my memory while I still could. Now there would be another before and after: before and after Dr. Mulder.

With Dad pushing my wheelchair, I rolled down the hallway. The medical assistants, the nurses, the receptionists, and the residents were all there, cheering, clapping, and congratulating me. It was crazy, because I should have been the one applauding them, thanking them for showing me a kind of compassion I hadn't known existed, and for giving me the strength to endure the pain. And there were more surprises to come. When I got down to the lobby, I was amazed.

There were journalists, TV cameras, flashes going off everywhere, a police escort, and a hundred strangers from all over the city congratulating me. I started to cry, overwhelmed by all this attention, and the tears flowed again in the car when I realized they weren't applauding because I'd almost reached the finish line—they were applauding because I'd survived.

4

After her audition, Chloe felt like spending some time on Madison Avenue. Maybe she'd find a dress or a cute top and make her mother happy, or, even better, make herself happy. She looked in the shop windows and browsed through a couple stores but decided not to buy anything. The air was filled with that spirit-lifting springtime scent, the sidewalk was clear, and her audition had gone well—she had every reason to be happy without wasting money. She rolled through Madison Square Park. From north to south, 5th Avenue gradually sloped down, so she could easily return home on her own.

When she appeared under the awning, Deepak rushed out to open the door for her and escorted her to the elevator.

"Your office or your apartment?" he asked, his hand on the handle.

"Home, please."

The elevator ascended.

"I got the job, Deepak. Taping starts next week," Chloe told him at the second floor.

"Congratulations. Is it a good job?" he asked at the third.

"I love the book."

"Well, I should start reading it—or, actually, no, I'll wait and listen to it," he said at the fourth floor.

"The man who was in the elevator earlier—is he a client of Mr. Groomlat's?"

"I don't remember every visitor."

They passed the sixth floor in silence.

"You remember, he received the package for the Clercs, and he got me a cab."

Deepak pretended to be deep in thought all the way to the eighth floor.

"I didn't really notice him. But he did seem courteous and helpful."

"I think he was Indian."

Ninth floor. Deepak stopped the elevator and opened the gate.

"It's my policy never to ask the people who get into my elevator questions, and certainly not about their ethnicity. That would be very inappropriate."

He said a quick goodbye to Chloe and returned to the lobby.

◆ ◆ ◆

Sam put the receiver back in the cradle apprehensively. His boss wanted to see him right away. Being summoned like this did not bode well. Sam tried to think of what he could have done wrong. But there was no time to reflect—Gerald, his employer's secretary, was knocking on the glass divider and pointing theatrically at his watch. Sam grabbed a notepad and pencil and trudged down the hallway with leaden feet.

Mr. Ward was on the phone. He didn't ask Sam to have a seat. In fact, he turned his back to him, spinning his chair to face the bay window overlooking Washington Square Park. Sam heard him apologize profusely and promise that action would be taken. Mr. Ward hung up the phone and turned to face him.

"There you are!" he shouted.

Definitely not a good start, thought Sam.

"You wanted to see me?"

"Have you lost your mind?"

"No," said Sam, tapping his head.

"I suggest you drop the jokes. You're funny sometimes, but not today."

"What's going on?" Sam asked timidly.

"Who is this bum that you introduced to one of our most important investors this morning?"

Sam pieced it together, thinking suddenly of Sanji's dazed face and disheveled appearance when he'd shown up late to their meeting.

"It's a very promising project with significant growth potential."

"A dating site in India? What's next? A strip club in Bangladesh?"

"It's not what you think," mumbled Sam.

"You're right, it's not what I think, it's what our client thinks. 'I'm one of the biggest investors in your firm, and I have always been convinced that we share certain values, and I don't mean just financial values, but ethical values,' blah, blah, blah. I'll spare you the unpleasant details and just share his parting words with you: 'I don't want to see this clown again!' This after a fifteen-minute conversation! I hope you understand my friend's position."

"It's extremely clear," Sam said stoically.

"So scrap the project!" ordered Mr. Ward, dismissing him with a finger pointed at the door.

Sam left the office and bumped right into Gerald, who looked jubilant.

"Someone just got in trouble," he sneered.

"Classy. If you spent a little more on your clothes, you might even look it."

"A true gentleman's worth is on the inside," Gerald snapped.

"Well, yours is very deep down, my friend."

Gerald was fuming, but Sam didn't care. He had put up with too much flak from his boss for too long. Every morning, he came to work full of energy and enthusiasm. By the end of the day, he was full of frustration and anger. He'd had enough. He recalled an Indian proverb that Sanji used to repeat when they were at Oxford: "It's incredible how many straws can pile up on a camel's back without breaking it."

"Was that really a proverb? Or did he just read it in a book somewhere?" Sam muttered as Gerald stared at him wondering what on earth he was talking about.

Now the camel's back was actually at the breaking point, and Sam decided he had nothing to lose but his pride. He abruptly pushed Gerald out of the way and burst back into Mr. Ward's office.

"Just one question: When your friend invests his money in a weapons dealer, or when, right after an election, he puts a lot of cash into a chemical company that's known to be one of the biggest polluters on the planet, does he worry about the morality of his actions?"

Sam plopped into the chair across from his stunned boss.

"Are you familiar with yin and yang? The flipping of a coin to guess heads or tails? You'll see where I'm going with this. Did you know that the two clowns who invented the cell phone in your hand started their research in a garage, scavenging defective parts from the trash cans at Lockheed? Were they garbagemen or geniuses? Let me tell you a few things about the person you called a bum—and some bums are very nice people, by the way. Sanji comes from a family that has more money than this investment firm is worth. Their house is like a palace. His father died when he was twelve. His uncles raised him. When he turned eighteen, they sent him to Oxford, and that's where we met. When he returned to India, Sanji discovered two things. The first was in his father's will. Because of his uncles' scheming, he couldn't touch his inheritance until he turned thirty. His inheritance is a hotel complex in the middle of Mumbai. The second thing Sanji discovered, or suddenly understood, was that his uncles had been cruel to him during his adolescence with one goal in mind: keeping him from managing the palace that they had taken over. And they were determined to extend their control over him into his adulthood. Basically, they tried to run his life as they saw fit. When he got back from Oxford, Sanji could have just kept quiet for a few more years and waited to get his hands on his fortune, but he told his uncles to get lost, and went his own way. You might be thinking that he was just flexing his muscles without any real consequences, but when you don't have a penny to your name and you're out on the street, and the street is in Mumbai, the consequences are very real. You weren't exactly wrong when you called him a bum, because he spent many nights sleeping without a roof over his head. But my friend is a fighter. He found odd jobs, got a place to live, and never let go of his incredible thirst for knowledge. He's curious about everything, and afraid of nothing. I think that's what I admire most about him. When he was a bartender, he ran into an old friend from school. This friend had a crazy idea, Sanji developed it, and this idea turned into a business—a very successful business. So now the question is quite simple. How many guys like your big client walked right past that famous garage where two young hippie-looking guys were playing around with defective parts, and today regret that they didn't stop? Sanji has his shares in the Mumbai Palace Hotel, and if he used them as security, he wouldn't even need our services. But he doesn't want to do anything to upset his uncles. If I'd gone through one-tenth of what they put him through, I would happily tell those uncles to go jump off a bridge. But not Sanji. Apparently, in India, respecting one's elders is still important. I can't help but think this code of honor is criminally masochistic. Actually, it kind of reminds me of my relationship with you for all these years. So now let's put our cards on the table. Do you want to go into that garage or not? If the answer is no, then I'll clean out my desk today."

Mr. Ward scrutinized Sam deliberately and curiously. Then he spun his chair toward the bay window, turning his back on his employee.

"Bring me the project, I'll take another look at it."

"There's no need, that's what you pay me for."

"You believe in this enough to stake your job on it? You know, if this ends badly, your career will be over, and not just here."

"And if it ends really well and is your gateway into the Indian market, I expect you'll find some way to show your gratitude."

Mr. Ward turned his chair halfway around and squinted at Sam.

"Get out of here before I change my mind."

◆ ◆ ◆

Sam told Sanji he had had a promising conversation with his boss, without getting into specifics. When someone like Mr. Ward threw his support behind a project, it was worth celebrating.

"Could you arrive on time for once, and dress normally?" begged Sam.

"Ten minutes doesn't really count as being late."

"Yesterday it was two hours!"

"Okay, but that was for a good reason. I had to help a woman get to a very important appointment."

"*Our* appointment was important! Do I know this woman?"

"No. I don't either, actually."

Sam looked at him, stunned.

"That just proves it, you're a total lunatic!"

"If you had seen her, you wouldn't say that," Sanji replied.

"What's she like?"

Sanji left without answering.

In front of the building where his uncle worked, he lifted his head toward the ninth-floor windows and hoped that Chloe had gotten the role. At Union Square, in the midst of a blaring symphony of car horns, he gave up looking for a cab and headed down into the subway.

He got out in Spanish Harlem. Here, there were no stone apartment buildings, no awnings over the sidewalk, and certainly no doormen in uniform. Plain red- or white-brick buildings stood alongside large housing projects. The smells, the colors, the worn façades, the deep potholes, the trash littering the sidewalk, the many different languages being spoken, it was a brilliant scene reminiscent of the streets he knew as a youth.

Back at the apartment, Sanji found Lali sitting on the sofa in the living room, slouched over her needlepoint and screwing up her face to try to keep her glasses from slipping down her nose, while Deepak was setting the table in the kitchen.

"Will you be eating with us?" Deepak asked by way of greeting.

"How about I take you out to dinner?"

"But it's not Thursday, last I checked," Deepak replied.

"What a nice idea," Lali interjected. "Maybe we can try someplace new?" she added, shooting her husband a look.

"I'd love to eat some typical American food," Sanji suggested.

Deepak sighed deeply and put the plates back in the sideboard. He grabbed his jacket from the coatrack and waited. Lali put down her needlepoint and winked at her nephew.

"It's three blocks from here," Deepak announced as they set off down the street.

At the intersection, Lali crossed the street as the light was just turning red. Deepak stayed back, grabbing his nephew by the collar.

"Did everything go okay with Miss Chloe?"

"I got her a cab. Why?"

"No reason . . . It's just that she was asking questions about you."

"What kind of questions?"

"That's none of your business."

"How is that none of my business?"

"My elevator is a confessional—everything that happens there is confidential."

The light turned green, and Deepak walked off as if nothing had happened. A bit later, he stopped before the colorful window of Camaradas.

"In this neighborhood, the local cuisine is Puerto Rican," he said as he pushed open the door.

◆ ◆ ◆

At 12 5th Avenue, Mr. Rivera put his radio under the desk. He turned the dial to a hockey game and began reading a detective novel. The night was his.

The Bronsteins had gotten home a while ago.

On the eighth floor, the Williamses had ordered in: Chinese for Mr. Williams, who was working on a news story in his office, and Italian for Mrs. Williams, who was sketching in hers. Mr. Rivera couldn't help but notice that their xenophobia didn't prevent them from enjoying foreign cuisine.

As the elevator passed the seventh floor, the sound of the Clercs' TV could be heard. They turned up the volume whenever they made love.

The Hayakawas had left the city in early spring to go to their house in Carmel, and would not be back until the fall.

Mr. Morrison, the owner of the apartment on the fourth floor, was at the opera or the theater, like he was every night. Every night, he would also have dinner at Le Bilboquet and come home smashed around eleven.

The Zeldoffs never went out, except to go to church. Mrs. Zeldoff was reading a book about the history of the Mormons out loud, and Mr. Zeldoff was listening in devout boredom.

As for Mr. Groomlat, he had left his office ages ago. He didn't usually run into the other occupants, except during the first half of April when he worked late into the night, his "peak season," as he called it, and in December, when he was angling for a holiday bonus.

At eleven, Mr. Rivera put down his detective novel, having developed a pretty good idea of who the guilty party was, and helped Mr. Morrison get home, which was no easy task, considering his inebriated state. He had to help him into his room, get him into bed, and take off his shoes.

At midnight, Mr. Rivera bolted the door of the building, slipped his work phone into his pocket (this way the residents could reach him at any time), and went up the service stairs. He arrived breathless at the sixth floor, wiped his brow, and gently pushed open the service door, which was ajar.

Mrs. Collins was waiting for him in the kitchen, a glass of Bordeaux in her hand.

"Are you hungry?" she asked. "I bet you didn't have time for dinner."

"I grabbed a sandwich before leaving, but I wouldn't say no to a glass of water," he said, kissing her on the forehead. "Those stairs will be the death of me."

Mrs. Collins poured a tall glass of water, sat down on his lap, and leaned her head against his shoulder.

"Let's go to bed. It's been a long day of waiting for you," she murmured.

Mr. Rivera went into the bathroom and changed into a new pair of pajamas that were waiting for him, nicely folded, on the marble counter by the sink. Then he joined Mrs. Collins in bed.

"They're beautiful, but you shouldn't have."

"I saw them at Barneys, and I was sure they'd be perfect on you."

"You'd think they were tailor made," Mr. Rivera replied, admiring the hem of the pants.

He slid under the covers, checked that the alarm was set for five a.m., and turned off the bedside lamp.

"How is she?" whispered Mrs. Collins.

"She was calm, almost cheerful. The doctors adjusted the dosage again. She thought I was the guy who painted the hallway and told me I did a good job. She still remembers she likes the color blue."

"And what about your book, do you know who did it?"

"It's the nurse, or the maid, or maybe they're in it together, I'll figure it out tomorrow."

Mr. Rivera snuggled up next to Mrs. Collins, closed his eyes, and went to sleep.

◆ ◆ ◆

Sometimes phantom leg pain would keep Chloe awake at night. But this time, it wasn't discomfort that kept her up. Sitting in bed, she was practicing her lines, adding gestures and motions that went along with what the characters expressed in the novel's dialogue.

She went back to the beginning of the chapter, adopting a low tone for the voice of Anton. In the book, the young stable hand was about to try to impress the girl he was courting. When the girl mounted her horse and galloped off, Chloe closed the book and put it down on her bed. She threw off the covers, got into her wheelchair, and went to the window. She looked out at the street awash with the rosy light of dawn. A man was walking his dog, and a woman hurried past him. A couple in evening attire emerged from a taxi.

Chloe sighed and drew the curtains. Her eyes fell on the book. She was an invisible actress, a performer trying to pursue her career in a different way than most.

She went to the kitchen to make some tea.

The water was just coming to a boil when there was a crash in the service stairwell followed by a shout of pain. The latch of the service door was too high for her to reach. Chloe tried but wasn't able to raise herself up with one arm. She pressed her ear against the door and listened: a small moan, then silence.

She backed up her wheelchair, quickly turned around, shut off the gas, and raced to her father's room. She banged on the door. Mr. Bronstein jumped out of bed and opened it, his hair tousled.

"What's going on?"

"Come on, hurry!"

She led him to the kitchen and explained that she had heard someone fall in the stairwell.

Mr. Bronstein rushed down the stairs. Four floors later, he shouted up to his daughter to call 911.

"What happened?" she yelled, furious that she couldn't find out for herself.

"No time to explain, I'll unlock the door for them!"

She rushed to her room, grabbed her cell phone, and made the call. Then she returned to her window and pulled open the curtains.

Her father was waiting on the curb, and she could hear the wail of a siren. An ambulance pulled up to the building. Two paramedics ran through the service door, following Mr. Bronstein.

She went back and forth between her bedroom window and the kitchen four times.

The paramedics came out again and loaded a stretcher into the back of the ambulance. On it was a man with an oxygen mask over his face.

Chloe waited for her father at the door of their apartment. He appeared at the end of the hallway.

"No elevator," he panted. "Mr. Rivera is in bad shape."

The Day They Changed My Bandages

Dr. Mulder asked me if I wanted to see my knees, explaining that some amputees wanted to and others didn't, so I decided to compromise and just look at one of them.

I knew what I had lost, but I wasn't aware of the extent of my injuries. Where my legs ended, my skin looked like a lunar landscape. I was in shock. Julius had left the room. Maggie put a compress on my forehead, and Dad went into the hallway with Julius, maybe to let us talk woman-to-woman or maybe so I wouldn't see him cry.

Then Maggie told me that, in the coming days, painkillers would be my best friends, but only for a short while. I shouldn't get too attached to them. I was fascinated by the good hearts of the people who treated me. Maggie called me "honey pie." In fact, my knee looked like an oozing honeycomb. Each time the doctor removed an inch of bandage, he asked me if it hurt. I have to admit their compassion was very comforting. If only I could have taken them both home with me . . . but my homecoming was still far off.

I held Maggie's hand, crushing her fingers as she told me that I was a real pro and I was doing great. When Dr. Mulder removed the last bandages, the pain was so intense that I threw up my breakfast. Julius had come back into the room, and Maggie handed him the basin. How romantic! I don't remember anything else. Maggie said that I had gone through enough, and she quickly gave me some drugs. She stuck a syringe into my IV, and I took a deep dive into oblivion.

When I opened my eyes again, Julius was still there. I wanted to know if I had slept for a long time, as if it mattered. What really mattered was knowing how long he had stayed with me. He looked at me closely and said, in a frail voice that didn't sound like his, that it would be a good idea for me to wash my hair. Then he sobbed, and I consoled him. He kept on saying he was sorry. Sorry for what? I told him he shouldn't be, it wasn't his fault. But he kept on insisting that nothing would have happened if he hadn't canceled our trip to Italy because of his work. I pointed out to him that I could just as easily have gotten run over by a car, especially since Italians are crazy drivers. Then he blamed himself for not going with me. What difference would it have made? I still would have been the one running the race. Why do people always feel guilty when something bad happens? Maybe it's their way of mourning for a life that will never be the same again. Before and after. Thinking of after, I looked straight at Julius and told him that he didn't owe me anything. He asked if it was okay if he washed my hair, with Maggie's help. Apparently it still smelled like 2:50. I didn't know how else to refer to what happened, other than the time my watch stopped.

5

At 6:15 a.m., Deepak entered through the service door, went down to the basement to put on his uniform, and came upstairs to start work. But, despite an ordinary beginning, this morning would not be like the others. The lobby was abuzz: the Clercs, the Williamses, and the Zeldoffs were talking with Mr. Bronstein; Mr. Morrison was half-asleep, leaning against the wall; and Mrs. Collins was frantically pacing back and forth. Only Miss Chloe was absent. All this excitement left Deepak speechless, until a puzzle brought him back to reality. Who had brought everyone down to the ground floor, since his colleague was nowhere to be seen?

Mr. Bronstein was the first one to notice him and came over with a downcast look.

"My dear Deepak, I'm sorry to say there was an accident. Mr. Rivera fell down the service stairs."

"What on earth was he doing in the service stairs at five a.m.?" exclaimed Mr. Williams.

"That doesn't matter now, we just need to know if he's okay," replied Mrs. Clerc, who had come downstairs in her negligee.

"What did the paramedics say?" asked Mrs. Williams, coming to her husband's rescue.

"Not much, but it looks like his right leg was fractured. He was conscious, though a bit stunned. I spoke to him—he knew what was going on," said the professor.

"Thank God. Let's hope he makes a full recovery," Mr. Zeldoff said in a low voice, discreetly ogling Mrs. Clerc's cleavage.

"I hope they do an MRI," his wife added, discreetly kicking him in the shin.

"Which hospital?" Deepak asked evenly.

"I told them to take him to Beth Israel. One of my friends is a doctor there," answered Mr. Bronstein.

"Okay, I'm sure you all want to get back to your apartments. We'll have to make two trips. Let's do this systematically," Deepak announced, like a ship's captain in the midst of a storm.

He did a roll call of his passengers: the Zeldoffs, Mr. Morrison—who was sleeping while standing up—and then Mrs. Collins . . . Deepak looked around for her and saw her rummaging about behind the desk. She opened the drawer, slammed it shut, and got down on all fours to search on the floor.

"May I help you?" Deepak whispered.

Mrs. Collins had just found what she was looking for. She got up and handed him a paperback book, which he quickly slipped into his pocket.

"You can count on me," he said solemnly. "Could you do me the favor of waking up Mr. Morrison on your way to the elevator?"

About one hundred vertical meters and a few minutes later, Deepak was finally alone in his elevator. He lowered the folding seat, sat down, and buried his head in his hands. He would have to let his wife know that he'd be coming home late. The residents would need his services to go home at the end of the day, and then he'd head over to the hospital. Who would operate the elevator at night? How long would the residents be willing to take the stairs after his shift ended? He didn't have any answers, and a vague sense of foreboding squeezed his chest.

As the day went on, life almost returned to normal. Deepak made his usual rounds. He took the Clercs' housekeeper upstairs, brought down their golden retriever, and handed it off to the dog walker. At nine a.m., Mr. Groomlat arrived in the lobby.

"You don't look yourself this morning," the accountant said as he stepped into the elevator.

Luckily his office was on the second floor and Deepak didn't have to answer.

At ten a.m., Mr. Williams needed him. Deepak was on his way to the eighth floor when Mr. Zeldoff rang. There was no reason to stop the elevator—people hated going up when they wanted to go down, so he picked him up on the way back down. Mr. Zeldoff and Mr. Williams greeted each other for the second time that morning.

"Seriously, what was he doing in the staircase at five a.m.?" muttered the Fox News commentator, who never missed a chance to suspect someone of something.

"I have no idea," sighed Mr. Zeldoff, who rarely had any ideas, except in the presence of Mrs. Clerc.

Deepak could feel their eyes on his shoulders, or maybe his hat. He was careful to say nothing, except to wish them a nice day as he slid the gate of the elevator open. The two men parted on the sidewalk.

A bit later, the Clercs left together, as always.

Mrs. Williams worked from home, Mrs. Zeldoff didn't work at all, Mrs. Collins never went out in the morning, Mr. Morrison never left before three p.m. when he was hungover, and the Clercs' cleaning lady didn't run her errands until lunchtime, after she'd finished vacuuming. Deepak had some free time.

He settled in behind the front desk, pulled the old phone book out of the drawer, and called the hospital.

This morning was definitely not like the others. Something else happened. Something that hadn't happened in a long time—so long, in fact, that Deepak couldn't even remember the year. The Bakelite telephone rang. Deepak stared at it, intrigued, and finally picked up the receiver.

"Have you heard any news?" Mrs. Collins fretted.

"I called the hospital. He's still in surgery, but he's stable."

He heard a sigh of relief.

"I know how you feel. Call me back on this phone between two thirty and three p.m. The lobby will be empty," he whispered before gently setting the receiver down.

Then his cell phone started vibrating, too. It had to be Miss Chloe. Back when the elevator was first built, no one worried about people in wheelchairs. The elevator call button was too high for her to reach.

Deepak went to pick her up on the ninth floor. She was waiting on the landing.

"I think it'd be nice for someone to be there when he wakes up," she said as the elevator descended.

"That's very thoughtful of you."

"I heard him fall, I was in the kitchen when—"

And, since this morning was not like any other, Deepak shed his legendary reserve and interrupted her.

"It's the boiler. It starts up at five a.m., and the steam rises through the plumbing. Since the pipes on the fifth floor are too close to the wall, they vibrate and make a terrible racket, as if someone's hammering the wall. You have to hit them to get the noise to stop. That must have been why he slipped."

"That makes sense, but why are you telling me this?"

"I think Mr. Williams is wondering why Mr. Rivera was in the stairwell."

He went outside with Chloe, hailed a cab, and helped her inside.

"Don't worry, a broken leg isn't very serious," she said, holding the door open.

"You're the last person I'd argue with on the subject, but at his age, it can be a big deal."

"I'll give you a call and let you know how he is."

Deepak thanked her for going to the trouble and went back inside, more shaken up than he cared to admit.

◆ ◆ ◆

Chloe watched Mr. Rivera sleep, facing away from the window. She remembered that when she was in Mr. Rivera's situation, in the hospital, after the color started returning to her cheeks, she would often gaze at the top of the maple tree right outside. She saw the seasons pass: the new spring leaves, the green fullness of summer, the ruddy hues of fall, and the black wood of winter.

A nurse came in to check his IV, and while she took his blood pressure, Chloe asked her how he was doing. The nurse hesitated before replying that he would recover full use of his leg. After she left, Chloe felt a rush of panic.

"Everything's going to be fine," she murmured, unsure if she was talking to Mr. Rivera or to herself.

Mr. Rivera's eyelids fluttered open, and then shut again with a wince. Chloe wanted to escape, but she felt frozen. She was about to call her father to come pick her up when a woman appeared in the doorway.

She was wearing a tweed skirt, a white blouse, and a sweater. She waited a beat, then walked over to the bed and smoothed out a wrinkle in the sheets.

"He's been a part of my life for thirty years, and I barely know him. Isn't that strange?"

"I don't know," Chloe stammered.

"My husband talks about him the way you would talk about a brother, a brother you see every morning and every night."

"I'm not a family member," Chloe said.

"I know who you are," Lali replied, sitting in one of the chairs. "He likes you very much. My husband, I mean. I'm sure Mr. Rivera likes you, too—you can't be all that different at night, can you?"

"You're Mrs. Deepak?"

"Mrs. Sanjari. Deepak is his first name. To be fair, he does call you Miss Chloe. I'll stay with Mr. Rivera. You ought to get yourself home—you look pale."

Chloe didn't answer. Lali stood and pushed her wheelchair into the hallway.

"I hate hospitals, too," she said, directing her toward the elevators. "Would you like to go grab a cup of tea?"

"I think I'd like that very much."

When they left the hospital, Chloe spoke up.

"Thank you, but I don't like being pushed. It feels like I'm being taken for a walk."

"You didn't mind before, so if it's okay, I'll keep pushing you a bit longer, especially since we have a few blocks left to walk, so to speak."

"Where are we going?" asked Chloe.

"I know a place with wonderful pastries, and since it's several blocks away, we can burn off the calories in advance."

"With you pushing me, I'm not going to burn off much of anything."

The strange name of the pastry shop was ChikaLicious, which amused Chloe. That, along with Lali's kindly air of authority, made her think of an Indian Mary Poppins.

"Why are you looking at me like that?" asked Lali as she tucked into a piece of cheesecake.

"Like what?"

"I skipped lunch, and besides, I love the cheesecake here."

"It's not that."

"I'm not how you pictured me?"

"I didn't picture you at all. Deepak is so private."

"My husband has known you since you were a teenager. He takes you up and down in his elevator morning and night, and he calls you a cab every time you need one, rain or shine. He brings up your packages, asks how you're doing daily, and your only excuse for not knowing about his life is that he's a private person? My next-door neighbors are Cuban, they have three children and two grandchildren, and the neighbors above us are Puerto Rican, she's a teacher and he's an electrician. There are twenty-four apartments in our building, and I know who lives in every single one."

"You might be surprised at how much I notice. If you only knew how many hours I spend shut up at home—though I actually prefer watching the people on the street to the people downstairs from me. But I can tell you that the Zeldoffs are religious fanatics—and bigoted to boot. If a light bulb goes out, they pray for it to get changed; if their door squeaks, they pray for Deepak to oil the hinges; in fact, they pray for everything so they don't have to do anything themselves. Mr. Morrison is a drunken dandy, an alcoholic with a taste for culture but no idea what's happening around him—a real character. The Clercs are a French couple who have lived in New York for a long time. They have an art gallery in Chelsea. I like them a lot. They're stuck in their own little bubble: very lovey-dovey, and they certainly don't care who notices. Mrs. Clerc wears low-cut dresses that catch Mr. Zeldoff's eye. My father notices them, too, actually, but you didn't hear it from me. Mrs. Collins seems to be a merry widow—she always has something nice to say. She used to have a bichon frise that barked all day long. When it died, Mrs. Zeldoff thanked God, but then Mrs. Collins's parrot started barking instead. And the Williamses—oh, the Williamses! They take themselves very seriously. Mr. Williams is a correspondent on the business desk for Fox News, so naturally he knows everything about everything. My father says he's a moron who thinks all of life comes down to business. Dad knows what he's talking about, he's an economics professor at NYU. As for Mrs. Williams, she's a crafty one. And such a phony. Every time I see her in the elevator, I secretly push my wheelchair forward to roll over her toes, and she's such a hypocrite that she doesn't say a word."

"You're really something." Lali chuckled. "If you're not going to eat your cake, can I have it? And anyway, what about you? What are you like? Sorry, I'm not as discreet as my husband, quite the opposite, actually."

"I used to be an actress. I studied at Stella Adler. I got some small roles and finally landed a part in a TV series."

"And now?"

"I do audiobooks."

"Do you work for free?"

"No, but it doesn't pay very well."

"So if you're a professional, and you're getting paid, why did you use the past tense? You're still an actress, as far as I'm concerned."

"Yes, but not the kind who signs autographs."

"I was a seamstress. Do you think I signed any autographs?"

Lali dabbed her lips with her napkin. The two women looked at each other.

"My husband will get home late tonight completely exhausted, but he'll leave for work at dawn as usual—maybe even earlier than usual. If I let him, he'd set up a cot in the basement of your building so your evening plans wouldn't be disturbed while Mr. Rivera's in the hospital. My husband takes his sense of duty to the extreme. I, on the other hand, am worried about what will become of us."

"The building will find someone to fill in for Mr. Rivera soon. I'm sure Mr. Groomlat is already working on it. Don't worry, everything will go back to normal, I'll make sure of it."

"Can you make sure that Mr. Groomlat doesn't convince your neighbors to go a different route? Times are changing, I know, but if things in your building change . . . if Deepak can't achieve his goal, he'll never get over it."

"What goal?"

"You'll think it's silly—I'll tell you about it another time. I have to hurry home. Don't tell him we saw each other. Deepak lives in a lobby and an elevator. He likes to keep his worlds . . . compartmentalized."

Lali let Chloe pick up the tab and left without worrying whether Chloe would find the right kind of taxicab to take her home.

6

"What do you mean they had to check me out 'at the source'?" Sanji asked.

"In India."

"They called my bank in Mumbai?"

"That's not all they did."

Since Sanji didn't seem to understand the situation, Sam made a confession.

"I had no choice. You come from far away with an ambitious project, how was I supposed to do this without any references? If you were American or even European maybe, but . . ."

"But I'm from the third world, a country full of bandits and slums, is that it? India is a modernized country that beats yours in everything except arrogance," Sanji fumed.

"With most of its wealth in the hands of a small number of elites."

"It's the same here! Success is impossible without the right connections! Whatever happened to the American Dream?"

"I didn't say it was impossible. But I mean . . . Come on, Sanji, raising that much money in just a few weeks—be realistic!"

"I only had one condition—keeping my family out of this. I'm counting on you to make sure this doesn't happen again, no exceptions."

"I wish it were that simple," Sam grumbled. "Your uncles trashed you. They called you a bum, a petty thief, the black sheep of the family, a pathological liar, and that's not the half of it."

"They called me all those things? So they still want war."

"It's high time for you to fight back. If they spread this vitriol in financial circles, all our appointments are going to end up canceled. Now, I just have to ask you one question. You can tell me to get lost if you want, or just fire me, but I have to ask."

"You want to know if they're telling the truth."

Sam picked up the briefcase on the table.

"Fine, I quit. You know what, maybe it's better this way. Do you think you're the only one whose future is at stake here? What do you think will happen if my boss finds out that I brought one of our biggest clients to meet a guy I believe in just because we had a good time in England and he's got a good head on his shoulders?"

"An Indian head," Sanji said with a bitter laugh.

"You've got to admit your behavior isn't making this easy. 'Where does your friend stay when he's in New York, Sam?' In Harlem, with an aunt and uncle he doesn't even know. 'Did his chauffeur drop him off?' No, he takes the subway. 'Why was he late for an appointment with our biggest client—?'"

"I guess I should have come in on an elephant. That would've fit the stereotype."

Sanji went over to the window.

"My uncles won't accept that I own a third of the palace and especially that I won't give in to them. My desire to exist outside the family is an insult to them. They want to see me fail—they want me to beg them to take me back with open arms. I don't care about getting richer. I want to succeed so I can prove them wrong. It's up to you to decide if you want to help me or not."

Sam chewed on his pencil, thinking.

"What's this palace like?" he asked.

"The standard. Four hundred rooms and suites, a conference center, swimming pool, spa, three restaurants, and very pretentious décor."

"Okay, so it's your standard palace. And it's in a good location?"

"The best."

"It's been in the family for a long time?"

"Not in this form. My grandfather systematically bought up all the apartments of several buildings in the heart of Bombay. When he died, my father and his two brothers evicted the tenants. They put the buildings together and did major renovations, and that's how the Mumbai Palace Hotel came about."

"How much is something like that worth?"

"Hard to say. There's the value of the land itself plus the profits from the hotel . . . it's a lot of money."

"And a third of it is yours."

"What are you getting at?"

"You're the heir to a palace that makes the Mark or the Carlyle look like small potatoes. Why did you take a twenty-hour flight to try to raise twenty million dollars from foreign investors when any bank in India would loan you the entire amount?"

"Because I don't want to take on debt. And if I'd had to put up some of my shares as collateral for a loan, I would've had to explain myself to my family."

"All right, I trust you. I'll put out this fire and reassure my boss, but you have to let me do it my way. In return, if I can raise the capital you need, you have to take me with you."

"Take you where?"

"To India, the paradise of new technology and organic dairy products! If your company becomes a major player in the Indian market, I don't just want a little commission. I want to be VP, with stock options and a penthouse apartment."

Sanji looked at him archly. On top of everything else, his friend turned out to be a hard negotiator.

"Fine, but no penthouse," he said, shaking Sam's hand.

◆ ◆ ◆

As he left Sam's office, Sanji wondered what his father would have done. Would he have taken his son's side or refused to cross his brothers? Still musing, Sanji went for a stroll in Washington Square Park.

NYU students were sprawled across the grass, children climbed on a jungle gym in the playground, chess players moved their pieces at breakneck speed, and a ballet dancer practiced her arabesques near the fountain. But missing from this cheerful scene was the young woman Sanji hoped to run into.

◆ ◆ ◆

Chloe stared at the only evening gown in her closet. Her mother had given it to her last year for a charity ball, begging her to make an appearance. The ex–Mrs. Bronstein ran around from one high-society event to another promoting the talent and success of her sculptor boyfriend. Tonight, Chloe would wear the dress for Julius. He loved Bette Midler, and she was starring in a Broadway revival of *Hello, Dolly!*

Chloe hardly ever went to the theater. When she did, she slipped in at the last minute, as the lights dimmed, so her wheelchair wouldn't block the aisles. Tonight was different. Julius was a good-looking guy, and with any luck, she'd run into someone she knew.

She grabbed the pole that she used to take down items from the top shelf of her closet and dropped the dress on the bed, scooped it up and put it on, all with practiced skill.

"Where are we, Julius?" she murmured to herself as she went into the bathroom.

She swept some mascara on her lashes, applied a little blush to her cheeks, and paused to choose a lipstick color.

A realization hit her. Frustrated, she went to the living room and called Julius.

"Are you ready?" Julius said. "I'll grab a cab and come right over."

Chloe didn't answer.

"If you want, after the show, we can go to that Chinese place you like—it's not far from the Shubert, we can just walk over."

Chloe remained silent.

"Is everything okay?"

Everything was not okay.

He was sorry to hear about Mr. Rivera's accident.

"That's a shame, but it's not serious, right?"

"I just told you, a broken leg."

"He'll be back on his feet in no time. I understand how you feel, but you can't get upset over every little thing."

"I don't think a fractured leg is a little thing," Chloe answered curtly. "But I was thinking of myself, actually. Mr. Rivera does the night shift."

"So?"

"So no Mr. Rivera means no elevator. I can go down and wait for you before Deepak goes home, but when I get back, we'll have a little problem. Well, more like a me-size problem. You'll just have to carry me in your arms, I guess."

This time, it was Julius who was silent.

"Never mind, it's too hard, even for my Prince Charming."

"I didn't say anything."

"I noticed. It's okay. I'll pay you back for my ticket, it's not your fault this happened."

"What are you talking about? You don't have to pay me back."

"I saw the movie with Barbra Streisand anyway. I don't really care about Bette Midler. But you shouldn't have to miss it."

Schopenhauer thought it over.

"I can try to exchange the tickets for a different night."

"You said it was a miracle you were even able to get them. It's fine, you can tell me all about it tomorrow."

"How long is this elevator problem going to last? You can't be locked up at home forever."

"You're going to be late, we'll talk about my logistical issues later."

"Is there anything else I can do?"

"Tell me what you're wearing."

"You're going to laugh . . . I got out my old tuxedo for the occasion. Maybe I can come see you afterward?"

"Have fun, Julius," Chloe said, and hung up.

She went back to her room and took off her dress.

Mr. Bronstein had been standing in the apartment foyer for some time. He opened the door partway and shut it again, loudly.

"I'm home," he announced.

He went to Chloe's room and found her sitting by the window.

"Aren't you tired of watching this street?"

"There's nothing good on TV tonight."

The professor looked his daughter in the eye.

"Don't say anything, Dad."

"I'll go see Mr. Groomlat tomorrow. This situation can't go on."

"It's not a big deal if I have to spend a few evenings at home."

"I guess you're right. I won't say anything, even though I'm thinking quite a few things. I'll get dinner ready."

Chloe turned to face him.

"What exactly are you thinking?"

◆ ◆ ◆

Mr. Groomlat was having a bad morning. He was even starting to regret pursuing the position of co-op president. Although Mrs. Collins had refused to sell him the office with the corner window, which he very much preferred to his own on the second floor, it was some consolation that he could wield power by controlling the building management. Up until now, he had had no cause for complaint. He enjoyed the title of president, and there wasn't much work involved. But this was too much. One after another, all the other owners had come knocking on his door, without having the common courtesy to make an appointment. It was always the same thing: When would he find someone to fill in for Mr. Rivera?

First it was Mrs. Clerc, whose dog had arthritis, and then Professor Bronstein, who complained that his daughter was a prisoner at night. The Williamses were worried about the party they were throwing next week. How would their precious guests get upstairs? And finally, Mrs. Zeldoff came to beg him to find a solution as soon as possible. Couldn't she just go back to her Bible study and let him do his job?

Getting hold of someone in the elevator operators' union was even more difficult than dealing with the DMV. He had already left three messages. Who still had an answering machine nowadays? Moreover, Mr. Groomlat had no intention of trekking deep into Brooklyn to visit their office in person. Who had time for that kind of nonsense? To cover himself, he would FedEx them a letter this afternoon, unless . . . He suddenly left his office. He called for the elevator, and Deepak appeared almost immediately.

"Hello," he said, sliding the gate open.

"Yes, yes, hello," Mr. Groomlat replied, not budging from the landing.

"Aren't you getting in?"

"No, I just have a question for you: Do you know anyone who could fill in for Mr. Rivera?"

"Unfortunately, his job requires a trained operator."

"So what is your union good for, exactly?"

"For defending our interests, I suppose."

"Maybe there's some retired elevator operator around who'd like to go back to work for a while?"

"Possibly, you'd need to ask."

"That's what I've been trying to do for hours now."

"I see." Deepak sighed. "You'd like me to handle it."

"That would be very nice of you . . . and would also be in your best interests."

"I'll do my best," Deepak promised.

"Please take care of it as soon as possible. I'm not paid to deal with these kinds of problems. In fact, I'm not paid at all!"

Groomlat went back to his office, and Deepak returned to the lobby, annoyed. He was way ahead of the accountant. And his friends at the union had confirmed his fears. With the frenzied construction that had overtaken the city, it was hard to find a regular doorman or super, much less someone who could operate an elevator like his. It was like searching for a needle in a haystack. If the union hadn't called back, it was because Deepak had asked for a small favor, even though he was aware that his strategy would merely postpone the inevitable. Fewer than three hundred kilometers left to make it into the record books. That wasn't much to ask from life, especially since he had, so far, accepted everything life had offered him without complaint.

He let an hour pass before going back up to see the accountant. He assured him that the union was aware of the situation and was doing everything possible to find a solution. In the meantime, he would extend his hours into the evening, in order to make everyone's lives easier.

"Work it out with Mr. Rivera so your overtime hours come out of his salary. The maintenance fees in this building are high enough already, as I'm sure you can understand."

"You don't need to pay me," replied Deepak on his way out.

Sanji recognized her from a distance because of the red pashmina over her lap that hung down like a gypsy skirt.

He sat down on a nearby bench and listened to the trumpet player's rendition of the "St. Louis Blues."

"I'm not going to break the ice every time we run into each other," Chloe finally said.

"You just did," replied Sanji.

"You don't seem yourself today."

"What makes you say that?"

"I'm a therapist."

"I thought you were an actress."

"For New Yorkers, it's a luxury to have only one job."

"Those are both interesting worlds. Though it's sad that therapy has become a profession—I guess the bigger the city, the harder it is to find someone who will listen to you."

"Were you just passing by?" asked Chloe.

"No, I was hoping to see you."

She turned toward the trumpet player.

"You liar, you're here for the music."

"I was wondering what my father would have done in my place. I'm searching for a sign," he said, looking up through the branches of the big Chinese elm.

"Do you think souls are wandering through the trees?"

"Up there or in another world."

"And what is the question you wanted to ask your father?"

"It's complicated."

"Putting our problems into words is always complicated."

"Wow, you really are a therapist!"

"And you believe in signs," Chloe said with a smile.

"What about you—what are you doing here?"

"I like watching life around me. There was a time not so long ago when I even hung out in supermarkets. Don't laugh! You can find all kinds of characters there—students, workers on the night shift, and elderly people trying to escape loneliness."

"You don't look like a student, and you're certainly not elderly."

"What was your appointment near 28th Street? You promised that if we saw each other again . . ."

"That's right, I did. It was a meeting with investors. I founded a company that has really grown, and I need help developing it further."

"So you're a businessman."

"An entrepreneur. Are you honestly interested in my work or are you just asking to be polite?"

"To be polite. Are you based in New York?"

"In Mumbai. I built an Indian version of Facebook—one that's much better than the original," Sanji added proudly. "Did you get the role?"

"Yes."

"A big role?"

"Huge! I play ten characters."

"You'll spend a lot of time getting into costume."

"I act without costumes. I'm an actress, but the audience never sees me."

"How does that work?"

"I record audiobooks. A voice with no images—the opposite of silent films, but I think there's a poetic point of comparison between the two, don't you?"

"I don't know, I've never listened to an audiobook."

The sky had turned gray, and a gentle rain began to trickle down the leaves of the big Chinese elm above their heads. The trumpet player put his instrument away and left. People scattered this way and that. Sanji looked up.

"Do you think it's a sign?"

"Did you ask him another question?"

"No."

"Then it's just a spring rain."

He offered to walk her home, but Chloe assured him that she didn't need any help and would get inside before he would. Before Sanji could react, she was already at the gate. She waved goodbye and disappeared onto 5th Avenue.

7

Mr. Groomlat dug through his files searching for an old invoice. Two years ago, he had suggested that the building automate the elevator. The manufacturer had a kit that was very reasonably priced. The elevator operators' salaries were a major expense, and eliminating them would clearly be good management, so he had been sure it would be an easy sell. This, however, turned out not to be the case. The residents were fond of the lifestyle that the old-fashioned elevator represented. Mr. Bronstein didn't want Deepak and Mr. Rivera to lose their jobs after so many years of loyal service, and thought it would make sense to discuss it after they retired. Mrs. Williams was concerned about the prestige factor, the Clercs didn't want the building to lose its undeniable charm, and to everyone's surprise, Mrs. Collins flew into a terrible rage and refused to hear another word on the subject, storming out of the meeting and slamming the door behind her. Mr. Morrison had asked who would press the buttons if the elevator operators weren't there anymore. Since no one bothered to answer, he abstained from voting. The Zeldoffs made a mental calculation of how everyone was voting and decided to join the majority. So the motion failed.

The accountant had never told anyone that he had already ordered the equipment. He had tried in vain to cancel the order and ended up skillfully disguising the expense as part of the regular building fees. When Deepak received the kit, Groomlat claimed it was a set of individual pieces that he had bought for a good price, in case the motor ever broke down, and told Deepak to store the boxes in the basement.

Mr. Rivera's accident offered him the chance he had been waiting for. Pretty soon, the owners would no longer be able to stand climbing the stairs. In a few days' time, there would be a veritable mutiny. He would ultimately prevail, and everyone would praise him for having planned in advance.

Groomlat was meticulous, and he wanted to ensure that the equipment was still where it was supposed to be. He took the service staircase down to the basement and crept into the storeroom.

The metal shelves were full. After exploring the back of the room, he was relieved to recognize two big boxes under a heating pipe. He pulled them out to check their contents. The kit appeared to be in mint condition. Satisfied, he hastily closed up the boxes and kicked them back into place before slipping out.

◆ ◆ ◆

On rainy days, the marble entryway always got dirty. In the late afternoon, Deepak descended into the basement to grab the mop and bucket. He paused at the threshold of his storeroom, aware that something wasn't right. He finally spotted the two boxes, and guessed who had opened them.

With a heavy heart, he returned upstairs to clean the lobby.

A faithful servant, he stayed at his post, patiently waiting until all the residents had gone home.

At 8:30 p.m., Deepak put on his raincoat. The wet sidewalks glistened in the dim light. He headed to Beth Israel hospital, stopping along the way to buy a box of chocolates. Scowling, he pressed the elevator button. He made his way through the hallway, asked a passing nurse for directions, and knocked on the door of Mr. Rivera's room.

"Does it hurt?" he asked, seeing Rivera's leg suspended in a cast.

"Only when I laugh," Rivera replied.

Deepak placed the chocolates on the nightstand next to an old magazine.

"It's a fine mess I've gotten us into." Rivera sighed.

"It's under control. I can stay late."

"The doctors say I'll be laid up for two months."

"It's a miracle you didn't kill yourself in that damned staircase, so two months doesn't sound so bad."

Rivera sighed again.

"When they find out, they'll fire me."

"They're so worried about finding someone to replace you, they aren't even thinking about how the accident happened," Deepak replied.

"If the insurance company gets involved, they'll figure it out."

"Don't worry! I came up with a foolproof story."

"You don't look very confident for someone with a foolproof story."

"You have a lot of attitude for someone in a cast up to his hip."

There was silence. Mr. Rivera hesitated to ask the question that had been bothering him.

"In case you're wondering, she's very upset, but she'll pull herself together," Deepak said gently.

Rivera winced as he tried to sit up straighter in bed.

"Hold on, let me fluff your pillows."

"My wife must be very upset, too."

"I'll go see her," Deepak promised.

"It's okay; you have enough trouble because of me, and besides, she won't recognize you."

"So she won't even know you're not there."

"You know, the more I think about it, the more I wonder whether my temporary replacement should just stay on permanently . . ."

"Why do you feel so guilty, you idiot? Your wife has been in another world for ten years now, and you spend all your free time with her. You've worked your whole life, and even at your age, you're still working like a dog. Are you trying to punish yourself for allowing yourself a bit of affection for once?"

"The thing is . . . I think it's more than just a bit of affection," Rivera stammered.

"For her or for you?"

"For both of us, I hope."

Deepak pulled a detective novel out of his pocket and dropped it on the bed.

As Rivera picked it up, he blushed a little, and Deepak even thought he saw him smile.

A nurse marched into the room and flatly announced that visiting hours were over.

Deepak rose and put on his raincoat.

"I'll come back tomorrow," he said.

"You still haven't told me why you look so glum."

"The accountant was rooting around in the storeroom. But as I said, it's under control, I'm not going to let them snatch away my dream . . ."

He stepped closer to the bed.

"Feel better, and don't worry about anything," he said, patting his colleague's hand.

He nipped a chocolate from the box and left.

◆ ◆ ◆

Deepak had decided to confide in Lali. If he waited too long, she would hold it against him. But sharing his concerns without making his wife worry was not going to be easy. Her happiness was more important to him than his elevator and breaking records. After dinner, he asked her how her day went and also, innocently, if there were still manually operated elevators in Mumbai.

Lali knew it wasn't an innocent question at all.

The Day I Came
Back to New York

I refused to ride in the ambulance because I hate traveling by car. When I was little, as soon as we got into the car to run errands or spend the afternoon in New York, the outing turned miserable, especially for my parents. I don't know if it was the smell of the leather, the bumpiness, or my habit of looking in the rearview mirror to see what was happening behind me, but I always had to travel with several paper bags. Mom put them on my lap before we left, and Dad had to pull over frequently to throw them out when they were full. By age five, I was not allowed to eat before getting into the car, and when I complained that I was thirsty, my parents just ignored me.

Until I turned thirteen, we never drove more than thirty miles from home. At least there was one good thing about their divorce: Mom kept the house in Connecticut (she had paid for it), and Dad and I moved to New York. No more driving! The freedom I found commuting by subway and bus was paradise.

But motion sickness wasn't the real reason that I wouldn't go home in an ambulance. The train was how I always got home before, and I saw no reason to change, after.

When I reached the train station, I lost my nerve. No more hospital personnel, no more strangers applauding me, only other passengers who turned to look at my wheelchair, shocked to see I was missing sixteen inches of leg, as well as my two feet. But, really, how much of a difference does it make? Sixteen inches is only 25 percent of my height. I know people who have cut off more hair than that, and who notices? Seriously, what's 25 percent of a person?

8

The alarm went off at 5:15 a.m. Usually Deepak opened his eyes a few minutes before the alarm and turned it off so his wife could sleep in. He sorely missed his routine. And as nothing was routine anymore, Lali had already gotten out of bed.

"You're up early," he said when he saw her in the kitchen.

"I didn't get a wink of sleep."

"You should see a doctor about your insomnia," he suggested, sipping his tea.

"It's not a doctor I need but an elevator operator."

"Listen, Lali. We've been through worse, and we've managed to make a nice little life for ourselves. I wish I could have given you an easier life, a more comfortable life, but I did my best. If retirement comes sooner than expected, we'll get by. We'll just have to count our pennies, that's all."

"And you listen to me, Deepak. I wouldn't have wanted my life to be any different. I don't intend for it to change one bit, and I certainly don't want you to change. So, we are going to find a solution, even if I have to replace Rivera myself."

"Don't be ridiculous."

"Who knows your damn Maharajas' Express better than I do? I've been hearing stories about it for thirty-nine years like it's a beloved child of yours—I can hum the sound of the regulator and the whistle of the counterweight, I can imitate the bell and the squeak of the gate when you forget to oil it. I doubt I'd need much time to learn how to operate a stupid handle."

"It's not that easy, actually," replied Deepak, slightly annoyed.

He kissed Lali on the forehead and grabbed his raincoat.

"It's much more complicated than you think," he added as he left.

Nevertheless, as he went downstairs, he smiled at the thought that she had been willing to sacrifice her nights to help him.

Lali put on a nice outfit, looked at herself in the mirror, and left the apartment shortly after Deepak.

She exited the subway. The farmers' market at Union Square was full of people strolling past the colorful displays of flower arrangements and organic cheeses. But Lali wasn't there to shop—it was all out of her price range.

The Callery pear trees were scattering their white petals onto the sidewalks of 5th Avenue. Lali needed to walk for a while to put her thoughts in order and find the right words before arriving at her destination.

She stopped at 12 5th Avenue, took a deep breath for extra strength, and walked into the building with her head held high.

Deepak was closing the door of the cab he had hailed for Mrs. Williams. He immediately rushed into the lobby.

"What are you doing here? Don't tell me you've got that crazy idea in your head—"

"As far as crazy ideas go, you're really one to talk. I just came by to take a ride in your lovely elevator while I still can. You're not going to deny me that, are you?"

Deepak hesitated, but he knew how stubborn his wife could be.

"One ride, but no more!" he grumbled.

Lali mimicked the squeaking of the gate as Deepak closed it and hummed along with the motor as the elevator ascended.

"I'm not sure why you bothered to come all this way if it's just to mock—"

"You'd never speak that way to one of your passengers, so take me to the ninth floor, please, in silence. I want the same treatment as everyone else."

"Fine, a round trip to the ninth floor, and then you'll be on your way," he said decidedly.

But on the ninth floor, Lali asked him to open the gate and went out onto the landing.

"What are you doing?" Deepak asked, annoyed.

"I want full service, so go back down to the lobby. I'll ring for you, and you can come up and get me with as much respect as if I owned an apartment in your beautiful building."

Deepak wondered what had gotten into her, but he closed the gate and took the elevator back down.

He waited in the lobby for a few minutes. Confused as to why the bell hadn't rung yet, he returned anxiously to the ninth floor. He became even more anxious when he saw that his wife had disappeared from the landing.

◆ ◆ ◆

Chloe invited Lali to sit on the sofa.

"I'm going to make us some tea. I'll be right back."

The idea of being waited on in a luxurious apartment was so extraordinary that Lali let her do it. She took advantage of the moment alone to admire the view.

"This is my lookout," her hostess explained, returning with a tray balanced on her lap. "If you look from the very edge of the window, you can see the Washington Square Arch. Well, in your case, you have to bend down a bit."

"It must be wonderful to live like this."

"In a wheelchair?"

"That's not what I meant."

"Did something happen? Is Mr. Rivera doing worse?"

"No, I came here to talk about someone else, actually."

"Deepak?"

"Your accountant, on the second floor."

Lali told her about the kit that would toll the death knell of her husband's career. She wasn't sure why she had come to see Chloe. She had always managed to solve her own problems, but for the first time in her life, she felt helpless. She needed an ally on-site, someone to keep Mr. Groomlat under control while she searched for a solution. When she heard about the accountant's plan, Chloe struggled to keep her anger in check.

"I don't know how yet, but trust me, we'll stop him. Trying to fire him wouldn't work, he'd find some excuse. We have to discredit him. This can't be his first dirty trick—maybe I could sneak into his office and look through his papers."

"I don't see how you could manage that."

"Your husband has copies of the keys."

"We have to keep Deepak out of this. He's too honorable."

Chloe rolled back and forth from the sofa to the window and the window to the sofa.

"I pace back and forth when I'm thinking, too," Lali said, then added, "Oh, I'm sorry, that was insensitive of me."

"Don't worry about it. I'll try to buy us some time. And I'll talk to my father—he always has good ideas."

"Whatever you do, don't get Deepak mixed up in this. If he found out that I went behind his back, he would never forgive me."

"You could use the service stairs . . ."

"One accident is enough."

Chloe accompanied Lali to the door.

The elevator arrived at the ninth floor, and Deepak provided his wife with exactly the kind of service she had requested. He didn't speak to her or even look at her when she came into the elevator. He led her into the lobby, still without a word, and escorted her to the curb. He bade her farewell by lifting his hat and resumed his position behind the desk. As soon as he sat down, his cell phone started vibrating in his pocket.

"Another eighty-eight meters, here we go," he said as he ascended to the ninth floor again.

◆ ◆ ◆

Sanji and Sam walked through Times Square.

"When you really try, you're not half bad. Your talk was so convincing, even *I* was on the verge of investing," Sam exclaimed.

"On the verge isn't good enough," replied Sanji.

"Be patient. We still have twenty more potential investors to meet."

"Sam, we are racing against the clock, and if I fail, I lose everything."

Sam grabbed Sanji's arm.

"Wait, I might have an idea. Our investors are hesitating at the idea of putting their money in India. Well, what if you opened a subsidiary in the US?"

"We don't have enough time."

"This is the mecca of capitalism. It'll only take a few days to set up a company—I'll handle it."

"How much would it cost?"

"Just some lawyers' fees. It's nothing compared to what we would receive in return. But you'd have to put some money in to show that you believe in it. Five hundred thousand dollars should do it. That's not a problem for you, right?"

Sanji thought of Chloe, and, suddenly, the idea of opening an office in New York sounded very appealing. The only problem was that his money was not readily available. The only way to obtain the necessary amount was to borrow it against some of his shares in the Mumbai Palace Hotel. Strangely enough, antagonizing his uncles no longer bothered him that much.

"Okay," he said. "I'll call Mumbai right away and get the numbers. I'll have a team design an interface for the American market, and in a few hours, we'll know what we're dealing with."

"What are you talking about? It's the middle of the night in India right now."

Sanji suddenly noticed a smell and began to sniff the air like a dog following a trail.

"What now, for Pete's sake?"

"Mumbai never sleeps. Follow me."

"What is this?" Sam asked uneasily when the street vendor handed him an unusual-looking hamburger.

Instead of a meat patty, in between the two slices of bread was a mysterious object fried in orange dough.

"If you want to live in India someday, you might as well get used to our cuisine."

Sam bit into the bun cautiously but soon began to enjoy the taste of *vada pav*. However, a few seconds later, tears streamed from his eyes and his face turned bright red. He bought a bottle of water and drank it in one gulp.

"You'll pay for this," he said, gasping for air.

◆ ◆ ◆

The owner of Claudette's welcomed the Bronsteins with open arms.

He leaned over to give Chloe a kiss and placed himself behind her. Mr. Bronstein never understood why Claude was the only one allowed to push her wheelchair.

"Your table is ready," he said, "and the bouillabaisse is exceptional tonight, by the way."

"Two orders of bouillabaisse, then," replied the professor.

Chloe told her father about Lali's visit and admitted that she didn't know how to prevent Groomlat from carrying out his plan.

"There's certainly no excuse for him to buy this equipment behind our backs. On the other hand, modernizing the elevator would restore your freedom."

"You don't mean that! What about Deepak, and Mr. Rivera?"

"Well, that's how our neighbors feel about it. I'll vote against it, of course, but we only have one vote out of eight."

"No, Mrs. Collins will be on our side, and she owns the offices on the second floor, so that's three votes already. We just have to get one more owner on our side to keep the status quo."

"We could try to convince Mr. Morrison, but then it all depends on his blood alcohol level at the meeting."

"What meeting?"

"I didn't want to make you more upset, but Mr. Groomlat called an emergency meeting. He sent out an e-mail saying he'd found a solution to the elevator problem—now I understand what he meant."

"When?"

"Tomorrow at five."

After dinner, Chloe asked for the check, but Claude refused to take their money, as always, and escorted them to the door.

"Why are you so generous to us?" Chloe protested.

"I'm not generous, I'm grateful. Hasn't your father ever told you? When I opened my restaurant in this posh neighborhood, everyone gave me three months, tops. They weren't wrong. People came in to check it out for the first few weeks, but they didn't come back. If you knew how many nights we only served a handful of customers. But Mr. Bronstein was faithful. He said the food was good and encouraged me to hang in there, and he had a brilliant idea."

"I simply suggested that he consider the law of supply and demand," the professor jumped in. "For one week, I told him he ought to refuse any reservation requests and claim that the restaurant was booked until the next Monday."

"And next Monday, the restaurant was three-quarters full, which is not bad for a Monday. Rumor had it that it was impossible to get a table at Claudette's. That's all it took for everyone to want to eat here. Ten years later, we're always full, except on Mondays. So you'll always be my guests."

◆ ◆ ◆

That night, no one could sleep. Maybe it was the full moon.

Chloe practiced her lines until the early morning, occasionally going to the window to look at the street. Earlier, she had been interrupted by a call from Julius, who wanted to see how she was doing.

Mr. Williams stayed up late working on a news story. Mrs. Williams had to finish the last illustrations for her book by the end of the week, so she was drawing in her office.

The Clercs were recovering in front of the television after a session of lovemaking.

Mrs. Collins was reading a detective novel out loud to her parrot in the kitchen. She burst into tears when the police officer twisted his ankle while chasing a thief.

Mr. Morrison enjoyed a Mozart opera with a bottle of Macallan single malt until five a.m., when he collapsed onto his Persian rug.

The Zeldoffs had quarreled. Mr. Zeldoff was brooding on the couch in the living room, since the street was too noisy for him to get any rest. His wife was reciting Psalms in her bed to atone for having used some choice swear words.

Mr. Rivera read for most of the night. He was in pain but reluctant to ring for the nurse, since the nurse in the novel he was reading had poisoned her patient.

At 225 East 118th Street, Sanji, seated at the makeshift desk his aunt had placed in the blue room, was Skyping with his team in Mumbai, entering forecasts and figures into his laptop.

Nestled against his wife, Deepak was the only one who paid the full moon no heed. He was sleeping like a log, but he wouldn't be for much longer.

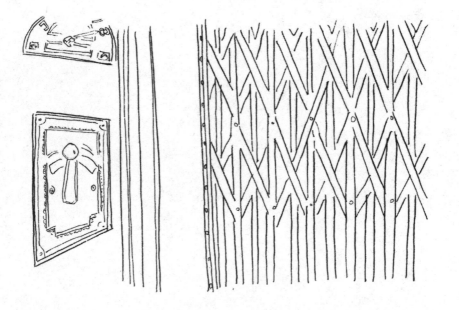

9

"What time is it?" Deepak mumbled, rubbing his eyes.

"Time to tell your wife what an amazing woman she is."

Deepak picked up his glasses and sat up.

"You couldn't wait for my alarm to go off?"

"I'm tired of tossing and turning in this bed. Get up, we need to talk. I'll make us some tea."

Deepak wondered if his wife was losing it.

"It's four a.m. and I don't want any tea," he protested. "I've known for a long time that you're an exceptional woman. I'm eternally grateful that you made me your husband. So now that that's clear, can I go back to bed while there's still a little bit of nighttime left?"

"Not a chance. You're going to listen to me now. I found a solution to our problems."

"You're not going to start again with that crazy idea of you filling in for Mr. Rivera?"

"Not me, but I know who can."

Deepak leaned over to look underneath the bed, then lifted his pillow, then went and opened and closed the curtains.

"What are you doing?" Lali asked.

"Since you found our savior by tossing and turning in our bed, I figure he can't be far away, so I'm looking for him."

"Oh, this is a great time to behave like an idiot!"

"You told me a hundred times that you fell in love with me because of my sense of humor, even though I thought it was my batting skills in cricket."

"Fine, so you want to be a smart aleck? Keep looking! You're right, he's not far!"

"That's what I was afraid of." Deepak sighed. "You're losing it."

"You said the problem is finding a qualified union elevator operator to meet the insurance company's requirements, right?"

"That's right, but I never told you that!"

"Proves I'm even smarter than you think."

"And I'm an idiot, because I don't see what you're getting at."

"Sanji!"

"I still don't get it."

"You can tell your friends in the union that your nephew is an experienced elevator operator from Mumbai, and they can sign him on as a trainee. All the union dues you've paid could be useful for once. And that blasted accountant won't be able to find any fault with it."

"Now I see what you were doing on the ninth floor. It was very kind of you, and I'm very grateful, but there's just one little problem with your plan."

"My plan is absolutely perfect!"

"No, it isn't. Your nephew isn't qualified at all!"

"He works in the tech world—don't you think he's got the skills to operate an elevator? Or maybe you're worried you don't have the skills to teach him? Teaching others is a duty you should have taken on a long time ago; then we wouldn't be in this mess."

Duty. Lali had hit the nail on the head. Deepak got very annoyed, which didn't bother her in the least, because it was the exact reaction she had been counting on.

"Let's say I train him," he said with a pompous air. "Let's say the union falls for it. How do you know he'll agree to do it? Unless you've already been plotting with him behind my back."

"I know how to convince him."

"I bet you can't. And we'll talk about it again when you fail," replied Deepak.

He took off his glasses, turned off the light, and buried his head under his pillow.

Sanji opened his eyes and grabbed his phone. He had worked so late into the night that the daylight hadn't woken him. He jumped up, rushed into the bathroom, and came out a few moments later wearing a nice suit. To make Sam happy, he had even put on a tie.

"So this is what status depends on in this country. And I'm the one who's supposed to be crazy," he grumbled to the mirror.

He called for a car and headed for the door.

"What a nice suit!" Lali exclaimed. "You look like a banker."

"I am meeting a banker, actually."

"Do you want to get together for a meal today?"

"I'm very busy today, maybe another day?"

"It's urgent, I have to talk to you."

Sanji looked at his aunt. Refusing her would be disrespectful.

"All right, I can swing it. I've got to run—meet me around five at Washington Square Park, on one of the benches near the guy who plays the trumpet."

"Which guy?"

"You'll know who he is," called Sanji as he ran down the stairs, too impatient to wait for the elevator.

Sam was on pins and needles. Sanji apologized as he entered his office.

"Is it a tradition in India to always be late?"

"In Mumbai, it is. With all the traffic, being on time means getting there within an hour of the scheduled appointment," Sanji replied.

"This is New York!"

"And since, in India, we never sleep, I have your numbers. I spent all night working on them."

"So let's hurry, then—our client is waiting for us, and he's the one you have to convince."

Sanji spent all day advocating for his project. The sun climbed above the East River, shone over 5th Avenue, and sank down toward the Hudson River.

At 4:45, Mr. Bronstein, who had let his students out early, was heading home across Washington Square Park.

At the same time, Lali entered the park on the opposite side, led by the music.

At 5:00, Sanji said goodbye to Sam, who was exhausted but feeling optimistic for the first time. It was not a done deal, but Sam could already see himself directing the finances of an Indo-American empire that would make Sanji's uncles green with jealousy.

At 5:05, Deepak took Mr. Bronstein to the second floor. All the residents were waiting for him in Mr. Groomlat's office to begin the meeting, except for Mrs. Collins, who had given him permission to use her votes against the accountant's plan.

At 5:10, Sanji walked through Washington Square Park. He tossed his tie into the first trash can he saw.

Lali was waiting for him on a bench.

"Here I am," he said breathlessly, sitting down next to her. "Sorry I'm late."

Lali was looking at the trumpet player's hat, which was lying on the ground.

"Did my brother keep up with the clarinet?"

"All his life."

"He used to go on about jazz when we were young. Now, when I hear jazz music, it brings back memories."

"Good memories?"

"I see my reflection in the mirror, and I don't recognize myself. I'm still the girl who would skip down the streets of Mumbai. I so loved to break the rules, to be free."

"Was life really that hard?"

"It was difficult. It always is when you feel different."

"Did you ever think of going back?"

"I dreamed about it every day, and I still sometimes dream about it, but there was a time when it was too risky for Deepak."

"You could've come back for a vacation."

"And find what? Doors slammed in our faces? A family that refused to see me and get to know the man I love? Losing your parents is terrible, but it's the natural order of things. When they reject you . . . that's truly cruel. How can respect for traditions be stronger than a parent's love? My youth was filled with lies and silence. My family's backward attitude was hateful, all under the pretext of religion."

"I think I know what you mean."

"You don't know the first thing about it. You're a man, and from an upper caste—you're completely free. My father sent me away because he was ashamed of his own daughter, and my brothers let him do it. All the same, we do have one thing in common: you and I are the only family we have left."

"A few days ago, we didn't even know each other."

"Oh, I think you knew me a lot better than you realize. It's no coincidence that we met. When you needed support from your family, you turned to me, because you knew that I was the only one who would help you, didn't you?"

"Probably . . ."

"I'm glad to hear that, because now I need you to do a little favor for me."

"Sure, what do you need?"

"Wait until you know what you're agreeing to! You know that Deepak's colleague broke his leg. Well, his accident has also had repercussions for us. His employers want to exploit this situation to modernize the elevator."

Sanji could not see what it had to do with him.

"I hope that, after all his years of service, they will compensate Deepak fairly," he replied.

"The richer people are, the cheaper they seem to be. Maybe that's why they're rich. But for Deepak, it's not an issue of money, it's his pride and his life that are at stake."

"But what does his honor have to do with it? It's not his fault."

"Deepak was an exceptional cricket player. The national team had its eye on him. He could've turned pro, and it would have been a gateway to overcoming social barriers and being admired by all. But we had to leave. Instead of becoming an elite athlete, he became an elevator operator in a foreign city. Can you imagine what that was like for him? So, to keep his dignity, your uncle got the idea of achieving something extraordinary."

"At cricket?"

"More like mountain climbing. Going three thousand times the height of Mount Nanda Devi on his confounded elevator. He's been hanging on to this dream for thirty-nine years, but his employers want to take it away from him, when he's so close to reaching his goal. I can't let them do it."

"Why three thousand times?"

"Why not?"

Sanji looked at his aunt with amusement, then surprise, as he realized that she was completely serious.

"And how can I help him cover three thousand times the height of the Nanda Devi? I get dizzy going up a ladder."

"By replacing Mr. Rivera for a while."

The trumpet player finished his song, put away his instrument, and gathered the coins that passersby had tossed into his hat.

"Lali, I haven't told you everything. I have my own company in Mumbai. I'm responsible for over a hundred employees. I came to New York to expand my business."

"So you're too important to play elevator operator for a little while, is that it?"

"That's not what I meant."

"That's what you said."

"I'm not too important, I'm too busy."

"Your work matters more to you than helping your family?"

"Don't twist my words. Put yourself in my shoes. How can I manage my business while working an elevator at night?"

"Let me ask you a question. What do you know about your employees? Do you know their wives, their children's names, their birthdays, their habits, their joys, their pains?"

"How could I? I told you, there are over a hundred of them."

"So from up on your pedestal, you can't see very much. Deepak knows everything about the lives of the people in his building. Most of them think of him just as the hired help, but he makes their day-to-day lives possible. He probably knows them better than they know themselves. He protects them. Deepak brings people together. What about you?"

"I'm not trying to belittle your husband's human qualities, and if I gave you that impression, I'm sorry."

"Give me one more minute," said Lali, digging around in her purse.

She took a quarter from her wallet and put it in the palm of Sanji's hand. Then she closed his fingers around it.

"Turn your hand over and open it," she ordered.

Sanji did as she asked, and the coin fell at his feet.

"That's what will happen to your wealth the day you die."

With these words, she left.

Troubled, Sanji picked up the coin. He looked up at the leaves of the large Chinese elm, and feeling even more troubled, he ran after his aunt.

"How many nights?" he asked.

"A few weeks."

"I hadn't planned on staying in New York that long."

"If you want to, you can, unless a man as important as you isn't free to do what he wants."

"I don't mean you any disrespect, but you are incredibly manipulative."

"Thanks for the compliment. The apple doesn't fall far from the tree, you know. So what's your answer, yes or no?"

"Ten nights, and after that, you'll have to find someone else."

"I'll do my best."

"A simple 'thank you' would suffice."

"You'll be the one thanking me. I'm sure you'll benefit from this experience."

"I really don't see how."

"Didn't you invent a system for connecting people?"

"How do you know that?"

"I did a Google on you."

"You what?"

"I turned on the computer and searched for information on you. For someone who claims to be in the tech world, if you don't know how to do a Google, you aren't very well informed!"

"It's called 'Googling.'"

"That's what I said. Since you want to connect people, here's your chance to really get to know them. Go and see Deepak. You have a few days for him to train you. As soon as we have your training permit, everything will be in order, and you can start work."

"What training permit?" Sanji asked.

Lali gave him a kiss on the forehead and left, clutching her purse to her side.

The Day I Came Home

When I got off the train at Penn Station, I gave up any thought of taking the subway. The New York subway I fell in love with when I first moved from Connecticut now scared me to death. The platforms were always so packed, I was afraid of having trouble breathing.

I had to learn to exist at a different altitude. My line of sight was now fixed on the torsos of the people moving around me. How could I be mad if they bumped into me? Ironically, the ones staring at their cell phones were the least dangerous: they walked with their heads down, and so I appeared in their field of vision.

Deepak was waiting for me on the sidewalk. True to form, he opened the door of the taxi. Even his "Hello, Miss Chloe" sounded the same as always. Dad handed me my board and went to get the wheelchair from the trunk. After unfolding it, he brought it as close to me as he could. I slid onto it, with Deepak watching, unfazed, acting like everything was normal.

"They're happy you're back home," Deepak murmured. I didn't understand at first, but when he looked toward the building, I followed his gaze. All my neighbors were at their windows, the Williamses, the Clercs, the Zeldoffs, Mr. Groomlat, and even Mr. Morrison.

Mrs. Collins was waiting for me in the lobby, as cheerful as ever. She hugged me and gave me a kiss. Dad wanted to turn the lights on in the apartment before I got there. Deepak took him upstairs, and Mrs. Collins stayed downstairs with me. She was quiet, but as we heard the elevator come *back down again, she whispered in my ear that I was damn beautiful, as if it were a secret just between the two of us, and she said it so sincerely that I believed her.*

Deepak grabbed the handles of my wheelchair, and I realized I had to get used to this idea that I didn't have feet anymore, I had handles. It was a significant realization, and it was Deepak who helped me understand what that really meant. We dropped Mrs. Collins off at the sixth floor. At the seventh, I saw Deepak crying. I took his hand, something I used to do as a little girl that just came back to me naturally. Maybe the height difference between us in the elevator had something to do with it. I told him there had already been enough tears that day. He wiped his eyes and swore he wouldn't do it again. And when we got to the landing, he didn't push my wheelchair. He stood by the elevator handle and said: "Back in the lobby, that was also the last time I'll do that. You don't need me or anyone else. Now get moving. I have things to do."

I exited the elevator. Deepak waved to me, and the dignity of his gaze made me understand that I was my own woman. No one would touch my handles again. Before 2:50, I wouldn't let just anyone take me by the hand—only Julius and my dad.

10

Deepak took everyone back home after the meeting in Groomlat's office. He had learned a long time ago how to decipher their facial expressions. The Clercs' sympathetic gazes, Mrs. Zeldoff's contrite manner, and Mr. Morrison's silence were as easy to read as the professor's crestfallen expression.

The main doorbell rang. Deepak said goodbye to Mr. Bronstein and went back down to the lobby.

◆ ◆ ◆

Chloe was waiting for her father in the living room.

"Morrison was the tiebreaker. Ever the diplomat, Mrs. Zeldoff managed to convince him that he would know how to press a button, even when dead drunk."

"It passed because of that Bible-thumper?"

"The Clercs were also on her side. If the kit hadn't already been purchased, I could have prevailed, but they wanted their freedom back."

"Their freedom?" Chloe cried. "They have some nerve!"

"They say climbing the stairs is bad for their dog's joints."

"And no one was mad at Groomlat?"

"It wasn't easy, but I got close to a year's salary for Deepak and Mr. Rivera. Our pocketbook's going to take a hit. Groomlat demanded that everyone pay additional charges to cover these new expenses. I don't know where I'll get the money. And don't even think about asking your mother."

"So, basically, our accountant hasn't only ruined Deepak's and Mr. Rivera's lives but ours, too—that's terrific!"

"I did my best. I'll have to go back on the lecture circuit. I'm not happy about leaving you alone, but I have no choice."

Chloe asked her father how much time they had before their building would change.

"It might not be that different," the professor said with a sad smile.

"But it won't be the same. We'll know it every time we get on the elevator."

"Yes, probably," Mr. Bronstein agreed. "But we still have Deepak for a few more days."

The light had faded in the living room, and the sky had grown dark. The sound of the wind rustling in the leaves floated through the open window.

"Great, I have to go back to campus, and I'll probably get soaked," Mr. Bronstein groaned.

Chloe closed the window. Big raindrops were splashing on the sidewalk. A delivery boy from Citarella darted behind a cart full of grocery bags, a man in a dark suit disappeared under his umbrella, a doorman in uniform hid under the awning of his building, and a nanny frantically pushed an expensive stroller down the sidewalk. Gusts of wind shook the branches of the sycamore trees, whirling the leaves this way and that, blowing away a newspaper that a woman had been clutching over her head. The window was blurry with raindrops, making 5th Avenue look like a turbulent Turner seascape.

"I'm afraid your old raincoat won't stand up to this storm. Your students are going to have a good laugh."

"My students always make fun of how I look," the professor retorted as he grabbed his keys from the bowl in the entrance hall.

Chloe barely noticed that he'd left. She hated the idea of her father running around the country in the sweltering summer heat, exhausting himself while Groomlat lounged in his air-conditioned office. She hurried over to her computer—she had an idea, and she needed to do some research.

◆ ◆ ◆

Sanji waited behind the wrought-iron door, soaked from head to foot.

"You're in a fine state." His uncle sighed as he let him in. "You can camp out in the lobby, but please drip-dry on the doormat first."

"I didn't come here just to get out of the rain. Didn't Lali tell you?"

"Yes, but . . . I didn't think you would agree to it."

"You're welcome, by the way," grumbled Sanji.

"Well, she didn't leave you any choice, did she? Anyway, follow me."

Deepak led his nephew to the storeroom and opened up Mr. Rivera's locker. Only his street clothes were there.

"Of course! I will get you another one."

"Another what?"

Deepak handed Sanji a towel.

"Dry yourself off and let's get started."

"I have to dress the way you do?"

"Didn't you wear a uniform at school?"

"Yes, but I'm grown-up now."

"You'll look better than you do now. As you can see, the cleaning products are kept in this storeroom. If it rains, like today, you can find what you need here to clean the marble in the lobby."

"It just gets better and better!"

"Did you say something?"

"No, nothing, please go on."

In the lobby, Deepak explained that he could sit behind the desk only when the lobby was empty—not in the presence of a visitor and certainly never in the presence of a resident. The front door had to be bolted before leaving the lobby.

"Way back when, there was a doorman, but it was too expensive, so they got rid of him. Soon, you'll get used to the different bells—the doorbell and the elevator bell."

"What if I'm in the elevator when the doorbell rings?"

"That's why you can't dillydally—you have to go up and come back down again right away. At night, it's unusual for two residents to need our services at the same time, and except for food deliveries, it's pretty quiet. Of course, it's more complicated when the Williamses entertain. The Clercs hardly ever go out, and the Zeldoffs never invite anyone over. Mr. Morrison always comes home around midnight—you have to look out for him; he usually can't put his key into the lock. Above all, don't start a conversation with him or you'll get lumbago."

"I don't get it, what's the connection?"

"If you don't move fast, he'll doze off in the elevator and you'll have to carry him all the way to his bed. And believe me, he's quite a load."

Deepak stopped in front of the elevator to explain the three golden rules of his profession to Sanji: be courteous; be invisible if no one addresses you; and if someone does speak, listen to the questions you're asked but never answer them. Then he slid open the gate and invited him to step in.

"This handle is the control switch. Push it right to go up, left to go down. There's no sensor when you reach the landing. It's up to you to gently stop the elevator at exactly the right level. So, when you're about three feet from the landing, you have to bring the handle back to the middle, then push it just a tiny bit to the right, and at the last moment, put it back in the middle again for touchdown."

"Touchdown?"

"For a smooth landing!"

"It's a little more complicated than I thought."

Deepak grinned.

"It's much more complicated. Let's see what you can do."

Sanji put his hand on the handle, but Deepak stopped him.

"It's better to close the gate first," he said with a sigh.

"Of course," Sanji answered.

"So do it."

Although Sanji pulled with all his strength, he couldn't budge it.

"You have to lift the latch and gently guide it so it slides along the track. If you force it, it goes out of whack."

"I thought this was the twenty-first century!" Sanji grumbled.

"A century of hopeless fools that can't do anything except type on a screen!"

They glared at each other. Sanji managed to close the gate and then took hold of the handle again.

"Don't forget to put on your white gloves so you don't have to wipe off your fingerprints every trip you take—the copper smudges easily. Okay, take me to the ninth floor."

The elevator lurched and took off at top speed. Sanji was terrified.

"It's not a rocket ship! Turn it two notches to the left, right now!" Deepak ordered.

The effect was immediate, and they climbed at normal speed. Halfway to the landing, Sanji positioned the handle in the middle, and the elevator suddenly stopped. Then he turned the handle slightly to the left, and the elevator went down about four inches. Then he adjusted the handle to the right, and the elevator went up about four inches. Then he put the handle back in the middle.

"Eighteen feet below the landing, not bad."

"You're exaggerating, it's barely four inches."

"Okay, seventeen feet, eight inches. We're at the eighth floor and not the ninth as I had asked. See if you can bring us up just one floor."

"I'd rather you show me how first."

Deepak gave him a satisfied grin and executed the maneuver perfectly.

"Fine," Sanji admitted. "It's complex, but I'm here to help you, so spare me your smug looks or I'm out of here."

For an hour, the elevator traveled up and down, first guided by the master, then by the pupil. Sanji finally got used to the sensitivity of the mechanism. His landings were far from perfect, but they improved after twenty round trips. He managed to stop one inch from the seventh floor and brought the elevator back down almost gently to the lobby.

"That's enough for today," suggested Deepak. "You should probably get going, the residents will be coming home soon. Come back tomorrow at the same time, and we'll continue your training."

Deepak led Sanji to the door. The rain had stopped. From under the awning, he watched him leave in the twilight.

"Don't bother to thank me," he grumbled.

He took his notebook out of his pocket and carefully recorded the 850 meters he had just traveled with his nephew.

◆ ◆ ◆

Chloe had decided. Her father's fate, along with Deepak's and Mr. Rivera's, depended on a stupid device that would be installed in the coming days. What had formerly been just a simple musing now became a plan of attack. However, she needed someone to carry it out for her. Her father would never agree, and it was too risky to ask Deepak. He would be the first one suspected and would need a foolproof alibi. She couldn't call on Lali for the same reason. While weighing her choice of accomplice, she planned to go the next day and buy the supplies she needed for what—according to what she had read on the Internet—could very well be the perfect crime.

◆ ◆ ◆

At noon, Chloe left Blaustein Paint and Hardware and went down Greenwich Avenue. The hardware store on 3rd Street was closer to her house, but it was the one her father went to when he needed to fix the toaster or a leaky faucet, and she didn't want to take any chances.

In a half hour, Julius would be having lunch in the university cafeteria. It wouldn't take her long to get there.

He was surprised to see her sitting at his favorite table, especially since he was with a young woman whom Chloe didn't know.

After Schopenhauer introduced Alicia, a teaching assistant he was working with, she went on her way, leaving them alone.

"Charming."

"Who?"

"The lady who serves the Jell-O—who do you think?"

"You don't believe that Alicia and I . . ."

"I wouldn't have assumed anything if you hadn't asked, 'Who?'"

"For your information, I'm quite annoyed that I have to give her extra tutoring when I have piles of other work to do."

"It must be terrible, I'm sure. But I'm not here to fight with you, I have a favor to ask."

Chloe explained what she wanted him to do. It was no big deal, she said. He just had to show up outside her building around midnight. He wouldn't have to come up, she'd toss the keys to the front door down to him from the window, and ten minutes later, after a quick trip to the basement, he could head home and no one would be the wiser.

"You're not serious?"

When Chloe remained silent, he pushed back his plate and took her hands in his.

"Ever since the elevator operator's accident, we haven't been able to spend a single evening together. Now you can finally have your freedom back, and you want to spoil everything? How long do you want to be imprisoned in your ivory tower, unless this is just an excuse not to see me?"

"My tower is on the ninth floor, not at the top of a medieval castle. No one's going to pour boiling oil on you. You only have to climb the stairs to see me."

"I've wanted to every night, but midterms are coming."

"Then what I'm asking you to do shouldn't be a problem; you'll have more nights to work. You shouldn't let an opportunity like this slip through your fingers."

"No!" Julius exclaimed. "Breaking the law goes against all my principles."

"Sometimes there's a higher law."

"Oh, please, don't use such a freshman trope. If you really want to play philosopher, allow me to quote Montesquieu: 'We do nothing better than what we do freely.' Therefore, I'm the wrong person to carry out your plan."

"I would flunk your class, and I'm glad," said Chloe, backing away from the table.

She left the cafeteria. Julius followed her into the hallway.

"It won't work—they'll know it's sabotage."

"They'll have no idea. I've thought of everything."

"They'll blame your elevator operator."

"He'll have an alibi because he'll be innocent."

"At best, you'll only gain a few weeks."

"A few weeks of peace and quiet for you, so what are you complaining about?" she replied, moving faster along the corridor.

"Would you stop it? It feels like you're always accusing me of something! I'm up for tenure at the end of the summer, and my whole future is at stake right now, so, yes, I'm working like a madman. When you were filming that mindless TV show, did I complain when you were away? Did I count the weeks you spent on the West Coast? No, I respected your work, and put up with being alone."

She stopped suddenly and spun around.

"My mindless TV show had millions of viewers. How many students take your brilliant classes? When our life together changed, you stuck around. But I can't be eternally grateful to you or feel guilty about it."

Julius stroked her cheek. "'We do nothing better than what we do freely,' and I feel free being with you."

"Save the philosophizing for your teaching assistants, and forget what I asked you. I wouldn't want you to betray your principles."

"*You* should forget this half-baked plan. Look on the bright side: when the elevator is renovated, we'll finally be able to go out at night whenever we want."

"That's very reasonable of you," she said calmly.

"Reasoning is my job," Julius replied, pleased.

He promised to call her that night, and suggested they have dinner together via Skype. Students were circulating the hallways, so he kissed her discreetly and then went off to class.

Chloe went along West 4th Street to Washington Square Park. She was disappointed, but, despite what she had led Julius to believe, she had no intention of giving up her plan.

◆ ◆ ◆

Rivera observed Deepak sleeping in the chair. He would gladly have let him rest, but the day had been extremely long and boring.

"Thanks for the book," he said loudly.

Deepak started and sat up straight.

"You know very well it's not from me."

"But you brought it to me."

"Aren't you tired of detective novels?"

"No, they're entertaining."

"It's the same thing every time: a crime, an alcoholic cop, an investigation, a love story gone wrong, and, in the end, they always catch the crook."

"That's what I like about it. The fun is figuring out who did it before the cop does."

"I'd like to see a writer who had enough nerve to let the murderer go free without anyone figuring it out."

"That doesn't sound like you."

"In a few days, we'll be done for, my friend."

"Then why are you wasting your time training your nephew if it's a lost cause?"

"Didn't we have a good laugh when I told you about his blunders?"

"We sure did."

"This may sound stupid, but in a few years, who will remember us? Who will remember what we did? Have you ever thought about all the jobs that have disappeared? Who remembers the importance of the people who did them? Of their hardworking lives? Take the lamp-lighters, for instance. Those guys lit up cities for centuries. From dusk until dawn, they went around lighting up the streets with their poles. I wonder how many miles of sidewalk they illuminated. It would have been a record by the end of a career. Then, one day, pffft! Blown out like their lamps, just dust in the night, eventually settling into eternal rest. How many people know they ever existed? But, you know, I think that there are still a lot of elevators like ours in India. When my nephew goes back home and gets into one of them, he'll have to think of me, and as long as he thinks of me, I'll still exist. That's why I'm doing this. To gain a little time before sinking into oblivion."

Rivera looked at his colleague with a frown.

"While I've been reading whodunits, have you by any chance been dipping into poetry?"

Deepak shrugged. Rivera called him over to his bedside.

"Want me to fluff your pillows?"

"Don't worry about my pillows. Take my uniform from the closet over there. Take it to the dry cleaners and give it to your nephew. Then his training will be complete. Tell him that the man who wore it is named Antonio Rivera, that he held this job for thirty years, and repeat it to him until this name is engraved in his memory."

"You can count on me."

"And bring some more chocolate next time."

Deepak went over to the bed, patted Rivera on the shoulder, took his colleague's uniform from the closet, and left.

◆ ◆ ◆

Chloe had just hung up the phone. Her father had called to say he'd be home late. Her cell phone rang again. She saw Julius's number appear and went back to reading her book.

In the chapter she was on, some friends were picnicking in Tompkins Square Park.

Her mind wandered from her reading. She missed her little apartment in the East Village, and so many other things that went along with it. Shopping at the deli on the corner of 4th Street and Avenue B, her favorite ice-cream stand on 7th Avenue, browsing in the little antiques shop on 10th Street, the fifteen-dollar manicures at the Chinese salon, the used books she would discover at Mast Books on Avenue A, as well as the wine store a few doors down and Goodnight Sonny, her favorite bar. She could have gone back to all those places, except for the wine store, where the doorway was too narrow. It wasn't just places she missed: changing your neighborhood meant changing your life. When was the last time she had gone out with friends? How many of them had come to see her in the hospital? Lots in the beginning, when she was on the news; ten or so in the following weeks, when the focus had been more on the perpetrators' backgrounds than the victims' fates; none after three months. Everything moves fast in New York City.

She could have tried to reconnect with them, but she had decided not to, perhaps because she was too proud.

◆ ◆ ◆

One floor below, Mrs. Williams was pleased that she could finally plan her dinner party. It was high time for the building to regain its splendor. What good was it to live in a posh neighborhood if you couldn't use your apartment as you pleased? It was so good that Mr. Groomlat had planned ahead.

"Do you think we should get him a present?" she asked her husband.

"Who? Deepak?" he replied from the living room, where he was reading.

She rolled her eyes and went into the kitchen.

"Do you want to go out?" asked her husband.

"And have to get back by curfew? No, thanks."

The Clercs were braver and decided to go to the movies.

After having dinner with her parrot, Mrs. Collins took his cage into her bedroom and put it on the nightstand where Mr. Rivera usually put his glasses.

She picked up the novel she had just bought. She wasn't convinced the nurse was guilty.

Mr. Morrison put a recording of Puccini's *Turandot* on the turntable in his living room. When "Nessun Dorma" began playing, he poured himself a glass of Macallan and went to look for *Fidelio* in his vinyl collection.

Mrs. Zeldoff called around ten to ask him to turn down the volume. Then she went back to bed and watched the rest of a black-and-white movie on TCM.

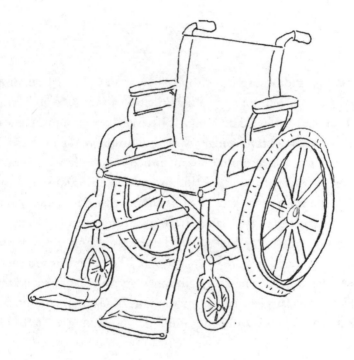

11

The recording studio was on the sixth floor of an industrial building on 17th Street. Chloe went up in a freight elevator that bore no resemblance to the elevator in her building. The elevator operator just pressed a button, so offering him the night shift wouldn't solve the problem.

Getting into the recording booth turned out to be not so easy. There were two sets of doors opening in opposite directions, and the passageway between them proved to be too narrow. The sound engineer had to carry her to the chair in front of the microphone. To avoid repeating this complicated and awkward maneuver, she decided not to go out for lunch, and just ate where she was. The room was too small for two, so the sound engineer thoughtfully suggested that he eat on the other side of the glass, leaving the microphones on so they could talk.

"That was good work this morning," he said, taking a bite of his sandwich.

The microphone amplified the sounds of his chewing.

"This is too funny!" she said, laughing. He suddenly understood and turned down the volume.

"I have a cousin who's in a wheelchair," he said.

"Oh."

"Motorcycle accident."

Chloe always wondered what drove some people to tell her these kinds of stories. As if having a handicapped relative would somehow create a bond between them. One day, when she was going to meet Julius outside his classroom, one of his students had told her it was cool that she was in a wheelchair. "I don't even notice a difference," he added. "If there's no difference, why bring it up?" she replied. Over time, she had gotten used to it. She realized that people didn't mean any harm; they were acting that way to mask their discomfort and dissociate themselves from the injustice that they were whole and she was not.

"It's great that you know the words by heart," the sound engineer continued. "But maybe you should just read it. When I close my eyes, I feel like I'm at the theater, but it's a book, you know. You have to take your time, just like a reader does."

"Do you read a lot?"

"I nod off on page one, but I've recorded a lot of books. Anyway, it's just my opinion, so it's no big deal. I'll clear away the trash, and we'll get started again."

He didn't have the gift of subtlety, but he was nice and he meant well.

◆　◆　◆

On his way back from lunch, Mr. Groomlat asked Deepak to stop by and see him when he had a moment. Deepak had no illusions as to the topic of the conversation, and he thought it best to get it over with.

"Things are quiet right now," he said, following him into his office.

Groomlat asked him to have a seat, but Deepak preferred to face the firing squad standing up.

"I couldn't do anything about it," Groomlat lamented. "You have to understand how difficult it's been for our residents since your colleague's unfortunate accident."

If he was hoping to establish a sense of solidarity between them by saying "our" residents, implying that they were both in the same boat, the accountant was way off base, Deepak thought.

"It doesn't bother me, I leave at the end of the day, but, for them, it's another story. I did all I could, but think of poor Miss Bronstein who's trapped at home as soon as your day is over. This situation just can't continue, and I haven't heard anything from your union. So they decided to automate the elevator."

"Was it unanimous?" asked Deepak, forgetting his usual restraint.

"Not the Hayakawas, of course, they're in California, and Mrs. Collins was a no-show. But the decision was made by an overwhelming majority," Groomlat noted regretfully.

"How much longer do I have?"

"Oh, come on, you're acting like it's a terminal illness. It's the exact opposite. You'll enjoy a well-earned retirement. A new life awaits you. I got you a fair shake. One year's salary! That sweetens the deal, right?"

"And what did you get for Mr. Rivera?"

"Six months, which is basically the same thing, because insurance will cover his salary while he's in the hospital."

"Not if you let him go!"

Groomlat seemed to be thinking.

"True. Well, six months isn't bad."

"He's been here for thirty years."

"That's the best I could do—you should have seen the looks on their faces when I asked them to pay additional fees to cover your retirement package."

"You didn't answer my question. When will the new elevator be installed?"

"Fortunately, the elevator repair people are available on Thursday. The work will only take two days. That gives you the whole week. I'd like you to help them—they may need your expertise. Come and see me Friday, and I'll give you your check. It'll be a nice windfall for you."

Deepak said goodbye. He went down to the storeroom with a furious urge to destroy the two boxes that were going to turn his life upside down, but it was only a passing desire, and he went back to his place behind the counter in the lobby.

◆ ◆ ◆

When Mrs. Clerc came back from the hairdresser's, she didn't ask Deepak for his opinion of her hairdo the way she usually did. The squeak of the gate and the hum of the motor were the only sounds as they ascended to the seventh floor.

When she went out to do the shopping, Mrs. Williams complained that her housekeeper had sciatica and couldn't come to work. When she returned, Deepak carried her groceries into the kitchen. She almost told him that she was having a dinner party the following week, but caught herself in time and kept her mouth shut, relieved she'd avoided a faux pas.

Chloe left the recording studio at four p.m. The afternoon felt like spring, but she decided to take a cab home. Sitting in the hot recording booth for six hours had worn her out.

When she entered the building, Deepak hurried over to take the handles of her wheelchair.

"No arguments—you look like something the cat dragged in."

"You don't look much better."

"I've been visiting Mr. Rivera every evening, so I haven't been getting much sleep."

With her, no pretense was possible. So, for the second time that day, Deepak broke one of the sacrosanct rules of his profession.

"I know you voted against it, and I'm sure your father did the best he could, so don't worry about me."

"Do you know what Lazarus said to Jesus?"

"No."

"'Get up and walk!' Not worrying about what's happening to you would be just as much of a miracle."

113

Deepak gave her a confused look as he slid open the gate.

"Isn't it Jesus who said that to Lazarus?"

She smiled, and resisted the urge to tell him that the matter wasn't settled yet. If Deepak were to suspect what she was plotting, he would do whatever he could to stop her.

◆ ◆ ◆

In the middle of a meeting after a full day of appointments, Sanji said goodbye to Sam without any explanation and scurried across the park. He quickly glanced at the park bench and hurried on his way. He was late. What on earth had possessed him to get mixed up in this nonsense? But since he preferred to look on the bright side, he told himself that trading this uncomfortable suit for an elevator operator's uniform would be something to laugh about later. If he had children one day, this would be a funny story to tell them, and perhaps it would even teach them a lesson. He was also amused by the idea of going back to Mumbai and taking one of those old elevators the palace was so proud of and showing his uncles that he could operate it himself, all thanks to their sister's husband. The irony was irresistible.

As he approached 12 5th Avenue, Sanji thought of the real reason he'd agreed to do his uncle this favor and wondered if he could have found something a little more subtle. How would Chloe react if she figured out that he had agreed to this crazy idea to be close to her? Would it scare her off?

The dry cleaners had dropped off Mr. Rivera's uniform, and it was hanging in Deepak's locker. He felt guilty about breaking a promise to his colleague. How would he explain the presence of a stranger wearing Mr. Rivera's uniform to the owners, since the elevator would soon be modernized? It would have been more prudent to end this foolishness, but Deepak wanted to have a little fun, and Lali was so happy thinking she'd saved their future that he didn't have the heart to tell her the truth. He would free them from the illusion when he went home Thursday night, after the installers had started their work.

Sanji showed up in the lobby half an hour late. Deepak would have commented on this, but he didn't want to push things too far. He brought him down to the basement and gave him a lecture on the mechanics of the elevator. The fuse box; the belt, which had to be checked now and then to make sure it was taut enough; and the oiling of the tracks. He covered it all, until Sanji reminded him that his job wasn't to maintain the elevator.

"What about your general knowledge? If a fuse blew, you'd feel lucky to know how to replace it."

"I don't know if 'lucky' is the right word, especially if I'm stuck between two floors."

"That's why you must always have this phone on you. By the way, Miss Chloe can't reach the call button on the landing, so when she needs our services, she calls this phone and lets it ring one time. You don't have to answer, just go to the ninth floor."

"The young woman on the ninth floor," he repeated slowly.

"You met her when you came to see me. You even got her a cab, remember? Well, speak of the devil," Deepak said as his cell phone began to vibrate.

"Go up without me. I'll stay here and observe this wonderful device in action so I can improve my understanding."

"Good idea," said Deepak, relieved not to have to take him along.

Deepak went up to the lobby and got into the elevator. He was surprised that his phone was still vibrating. He was going as fast as he could! He was even more surprised when he got up to the ninth floor and didn't see Chloe on the landing.

She must have called him by mistake. But just in case, before going back down, Deepak put his ear up to her door. He heard a call for help.

He took out the key ring hanging from his belt and entered the apartment.

"In the kitchen!" she moaned.

He rushed down the hallway and found Chloe on the floor with her wheelchair on top of her.

"Don't move!" he said, righting the wheelchair.

He picked Chloe up and carried her to the sofa in the living room. "Are you hurt?"

"No, I don't think so. I leaned over to get a cup from the shelf, but I couldn't reach it, so I grabbed the knob of one of the cabinets. I forgot to put the brake on, and my wheelchair slid back—by the time I realized what was happening, it was too late."

"I'll call a doctor."

"No need, I may have some bruises, but that'll teach me not to do acrobatics."

"Let me at least check that the wheelchair is all right. Goodness, you really scared me!"

A few moments later, he came back, pushing the wheelchair.

"Everything's in working order, I even checked the brake," he said in a soothing voice. "Do you want me to stay with you?"

"That's very nice of you, but I'm fine. Everyone trips over their own feet sometimes."

"You always have a good sense of humor."

He knew her well enough to know that she wasn't so much making a joke as protecting her pride.

"If I could do it," she continued, "I would pay your salary myself so you would never leave."

"Come now, you know very well that's not the issue."

"How will I manage without you?"

"During the last four years, you've only needed my help twice."

"Five times!"

"You gave me a lot more trouble when you were a teenager."

"Did I really give you a hard time?"

"No . . . but you were no angel. Should I help you back into the wheelchair before I leave?"

"I can do it myself. They say if you fall off the horse, you just have to get right back on."

Deepak said goodbye and left. She didn't hear the usual squeak from the front door as it closed. She called to him from the living room.

"I'm fine!"

This time, she heard the squeak.

◆ ◆ ◆

"It took you a while. I thought the elevator had broken down."

"Did you see any sparks on the fuse box? No? Then everything's fine. Let's get moving. A few round trips, and we'll see if you remember yesterday's lesson. Then I'll send you home, I have to leave a little early tonight."

"I always have the unpleasant feeling I'm ten years old again when I'm with you," Sanji complained.

"And I feel like I'm a hundred!"

The first trips were chaotic, but Sanji finally got the hang of it. He managed to get within a couple of inches of a perfect stop. An hour later, Deepak accompanied him to the door and recorded the distance they had traveled in his notebook. Between six and seven p.m., the residents returned one by one to their apartments, all with gloomy expressions. Their hypocritical attitudes were already bad enough, but Mr. Williams even laid his hand on Deepak's shoulder. Deepak brushed himself off and closed the gate without saying goodbye.

When he got inside, Mr. Williams told his wife that he wished they'd hurry up and put in the new elevator. Riding in this one had become a living hell.

At 7:30, Deepak went down to the basement and changed his clothes. Some might have accused him of abandoning his post an hour before he was supposed to leave. But no matter, he had a promise to keep. Once in his street clothes, he brought the elevator upstairs for its final trip of the day and rode it back down a few moments later.

Still recovering from her fall, Chloe had to handle another challenge. Going from her wheelchair to the shower chair had to be done very carefully. Except for the little incident in the kitchen, the day had been good. The publisher had come to see her in the studio. He had congratulated her and given her another book to do, saying he was ready to sign a new contract.

She would celebrate with her father, but not tonight. She was exhausted.

The hot water streaming over her shoulders felt wonderful.

After putting on her robe, she went to the living room and sat by the window. She was surprised to see Deepak get into a cab with Mrs. Collins. Then, suddenly understanding the reason behind their excursion, she had an idea.

The Day I Took the Subway Again

Taxis were costing me a fortune. I could only use the minivans that have a ramp and a sliding door. Unfortunately, most taxis are sedans—the driver has to get out of the car, load my wheelchair into the trunk, and then go through the whole rigamarole again at the end of the ride. Most of them simply ignore me when I try to hail them. Some of them even have the courtesy to speed up, as if they're afraid I might grab on to their bumper.

I headed down into the subway, thinking of my first euphoric trips underground when I moved to New York. It's best not to breathe in too deeply when you take the elevators, and they move so slowly that it's like descending into a cavern. I avoided rush hour, and when I got onto the train at West 4th Street, everything went smoothly at first. My brakes were on so I wouldn't go flying into the doors when the conductor halted the train. The car was almost empty, and the passengers, eyes glued to their cell phones, paid no attention to me. Things got more complicated at Penn Station. A crowd of people pushed into the train. My wheelchair took up too much space, and the passengers who were standing up had to press against me. I was surrounded by a ring of coats, shirts, belt buckles, briefcases, and purses that grew tighter and tighter. Suddenly I couldn't breathe. The train was moving fast, and as it went around a curve, a heavyset man fell into me and then suddenly regained his balance, griping loudly. Another charmer almost sat on my lap. I felt like I was suffocating. I panicked and started shouting. People are naturally on edge in big cities (I, for one, certainly know why), and when a woman starts yelling in a crowded train, the effect is immediate. There was a stampede, and I felt ashamed when I saw a mother pick up a terrified little girl so she wouldn't be trampled. Then a man ordered everyone to calm down. There was space around me now—I must have looked like a crazy woman. I was sweating, I was panting, I was trying to breathe normally again, and people were staring at me, a mixture of fear and disgust in their eyes. A woman forced her way through, squatted down in front of me, and told me to breathe slowly. She said I had nothing to fear and everything would be okay. She took my hand and massaged my fingers. "I know," she murmured. "My sister's in a wheelchair, and this has happened to her lots of times—it's totally normal."

I didn't see anything normal about making a spectacle, wetting myself, frightening a little girl who was still shaking, and attracting stares from everyone in the car. The idea that this would happen to me many times over was something I couldn't conceive of. Even this woman's kindness wasn't normal.

My heartbeat slowed, I finally became calm again, and people stopped staring. I thanked the woman who had helped me and assured her I felt better, but when the train finally stopped, she insisted on accompanying me onto the platform. She truly must have had a sister like me; she didn't even try to push my wheelchair. She just led me to the station manager. I wouldn't let him call an ambulance. I just wanted to go home.

When Dad came home from campus, he asked me how my day was. I told him I took the subway. He was thrilled for me, and said he thought that was absolutely wonderful and congratulated me.

12

Mr. Groomlat didn't have a secretary, not because he was cheap but because he didn't trust anyone but himself. He arrived at his office early and kept a lookout for the elevator-replacement crew from his window. He wanted to personally make sure that Deepak would help them with their work. The old Indian man might be offended, but to hell with being sensitive—he was the executive leader of the co-op, and he had a job to do.

When Deepak saw Mr. Groomlat arrive earlier than usual, he immediately realized his intentions. Groomlat was the kind of person who would have paid for a seat at an execution. He led the accountant and the technicians to the storeroom.

"How long will it take?" Groomlat asked. "We don't want the elevator to be out of service over the weekend."

"This is incredible," exclaimed Jorge Santos, the elder of the two technicians and clearly the boss.

"What's incredible?" Groomlat asked in a worried voice.

"I've modernized some of these old models, but this one is in remarkable shape—it's almost like new."

Deepak took off his cap, offering one final moment of silence to something he had cherished for so many years. Of course it was almost like new, you idiot, he thought. He couldn't have taken better care of it if it were his own child.

"Any last-minute regrets?" Jorge Santos asked. "After the job is done, we'll change the certificate and the work will be irreversible."

"You're asking *me*?" Deepak chimed in, a touch of sarcasm in his voice.

"Get it done," Groomlat replied drily.

"Maybe we can finish tonight," Jorge Santos said.

"What does this 'maybe' depend on?" asked Groomlat.

"On you. Given the excellent state of the machinery, we just have to install the electronic relays and the button panel in the elevator compartment. If we put the panel where the handle is, it'll be quick. But if you want to keep the handle, then we'll have to cut into the woodwork on the other side of the gate, and that'll take an extra day."

"Why would we want to keep it? It won't be of any use, if I understand correctly?"

"For charm. Some people get very attached to antiques."

"My wife, for example," Deepak said offhand.

"Let's limit unnecessary expenses. Remove the handle and give it to Deepak. We'll be happy to give him this nice souvenir."

Santos's coworker, who was kneeling in front of the two boxes, stood up abruptly. "There's one little problem, though."

"What?" Groomlat spun around to face him.

"Well, your elevator may be well preserved, but these parts I've just inspected have aged rather badly. I'd go so far as to say they're dead," continued the second technician, who, according to the name stitched on his overalls, was known as Ernest Pavlovitch.

"What do you mean, 'dead'?" Groomlat said indignantly.

"Oxidized, if you prefer. In any case, we can't use this junk."

"What are you talking about—they're brand new!" Groomlat protested. "They haven't been taken out of the packaging since we received them!"

"I'm not so sure about that. These boxes weren't closed tightly. See for yourself—the packaging was torn when they were stored underneath these pipes."

Groomlat's cheeks turned crimson. He noticed Deepak's amused look and regained his composure.

"Come on, can't you just clean them off?"

"No way, they've been eaten away by moisture," the elevator expert explained, displaying the whitish substance covering the electronic components. "Mm-hmm," he said, shaking his head. "They're shot. You gotta buy a whole new kit."

"Okay, you can charge me for it! Go get it and come back right away."

The technicians exchanged a mocking look.

"You think we have this stuff just lying around? It's custom made—the parts have to be manufactured, then tested in the workshop."

"How long will that take?" The accountant sighed.

"Twelve to sixteen weeks, minimum. Plus shipping time from England."

"England?"

"The only company that still makes this kind of equipment is near Birmingham. But they're very thorough, don't worry. Well, anyway, I think we're done here. I'll send you a new quote ASAP."

◆ ◆ ◆

Groomlat wasn't the only one watching for the technicians' arrival from the window. When Chloe saw them get back into their van, half an hour after they'd shown up, she knew her plan had worked. It only remained to be seen if the crime was as perfect as she thought.

◆ ◆ ◆

"Well, don't just stand there. You must be pleased—it seems we'll need your services a bit longer than planned," the accountant grumbled.

"Twelve to sixteen weeks, plus shipping . . ."

"I can only imagine how happy this makes you."

"Why would I be happy when my job ends tomorrow?"

"I haven't officially let you go yet."

"Yes, you did, yesterday."

"Watch out, Deepak, if you want to cash that check one day, I suggest you don't get smart with me."

"A binding contract guaranteeing eighteen months of work, with a year's salary when we leave. And Mr. Rivera gets the same deal, of course. Put it all in writing, or come Saturday, everyone will be taking the stairs, both night and day."

"How dare you blackmail me after all the trouble I went to for you?"

"Mr. Groomlat, I've been taking you up and down in my elevator for ten years, and I've never underestimated you. Have the courtesy to return the favor. You have until tomorrow to get me a signed letter from the co-op. My shift is over at seven fifteen p.m., and when I say 'over,' I mean it might be over for good," Deepak replied, leaving the accountant behind in the basement.

"What about nights? What will we do for the night shift during all this time? And what will Mr. Bronstein say when he finds out his daughter—"

"Leave the Bronsteins out of it—they can speak for themselves. As for nights, I'll see what I can do about it as soon as I have my letter in hand."

◆ ◆ ◆

Deepak waited for the accountant to go back to his office. For once, his morning had had more ups than downs.

At ten a.m., his cell phone vibrated. Chloe was waiting for him on the landing.

"Beautiful day, isn't it?"

"Yes indeed, although the forecast calls for rain in the early afternoon."

"A good rain will clean off the sidewalks."

"That's one way to look at it. Would you like to go down or would you rather just talk about the weather on the landing?"

She rolled in backward, and Deepak closed the gate. He remained silent until the fourth floor.

"Why are you so cheerful this morning?" he asked as they passed the third floor.

"I'm always cheerful," she assured him at the second floor.

Deepak preceded Chloe into the lobby and accompanied her to the street.

"Should I get you a taxi?"

"Not today, thanks. The Christopher Street station is ten minutes away, and I can take the one train to the recording studio, so there's no transfer. Don't worry about me, as Lazarus would say."

As Deepak watched her leave, he admired how energetically she steered her wheelchair, but was also just a tiny bit suspicious.

Composing this e-mail was one of the most humiliating experiences of his career. Mr. Groomlat had chosen each word with the utmost care, emphasizing that no one could have predicted that the automation kit would be damaged, not even him. He had reported the facts in detail, being careful not to relate Deepak's demands. As he reread his words, he swore to himself that he'd find a way to avoid honoring a promise that had been extorted from him. He hit send, and his e-mail flew off to its recipients.

A few minutes later, Mrs. Williams turned up in his office.

"You don't find it strange that this equipment, which cost us a fortune, is unusable and that we just happen to discover this on the day it's supposed to be installed?" she asked.

Groomlat cautiously moved his pawns forward. "Do you think it was defective to begin with?"

"I hope that, after buying it without our permission, you at least checked its condition when you received it!"

"Let's not play cat and mouse. If you want to criticize me, please just say so in plain English."

"Don't get hot under the collar," she said, sitting down in the armchair across from him. "It just seems as if there have been a lot of odd coincidences in this building recently."

"If you aren't accusing the suppliers, then who is to blame?"

"Ask the Clercs—when they aren't busy getting it on, they watch cop shows. Unfortunately, I can hear both their moaning and the sound of their TV."

"And what exactly should I ask them?"

"The motive! When you establish the motive, the mystery's solved. Who had a reason to keep things the way they are? I'll let you think it over. In the meantime, you simply must solve the problem of the night shift. I had to postpone my dinner until next week—I can't put it off again!"

She left without saying goodbye, leaving Groomlat pensive.

He called the elevator company and said he urgently needed to speak with Jorge Santos.

His inquiry consisted of a single question: What could be the cause of such significant damage?

The technician knew his stuff. Since he was familiar with his customers' tendency to always find a good reason not to pay their bill, he had a ready explanation at hand. Storing electronic equipment under heating pipes wasn't very smart. Condensation had probably oxidized the equipment.

This certainly didn't substantiate Mrs. Williams's veiled accusation of Deepak, especially since the elevator operator had never been informed of the contents of the boxes in question. But one detail did come back to him: he didn't recall having smelled the least bit of dampness when he opened them.

"Could this damage have happened over just a few days?" he asked in a low voice.

"I'd be surprised. I've rarely seen so much grime. I don't know what filth is running in your pipes, but I wouldn't drink that water if I were you. The relays were covered with a whitish substance, salt or lime," Jorge Santos explained. "I e-mailed the manufacturer. With any luck, they may have another kit in stock, or a model they could adapt. We might just get lucky."

Groomlat thanked him warmly.

◆ ◆ ◆

When he got home, Deepak suggested to Lali that they eat out, which didn't particularly surprise her, since it was Thursday. But when he cheerfully suggested they invite her nephew to go with them, she was intrigued. The last time she had seen her husband in such high spirits was when Virat Kohli, the captain of the Indian cricket team, had been named best batsman in the world by ESPN.

But they hadn't heard from Sanji, and it was already getting late. Lali preferred to stay at home and have dinner alone with her husband.

The Day I Started Physical Therapy

When I was acting, I never had a personal trainer. My career hadn't propelled me into that special club. But losing half my legs granted me automatic membership. The human body is an incredibly sophisticated mechanism. Designed to adapt to any situation, it conceals dormant secondary circuits—hidden treasures, ready to be unearthed when the need arises. Gilbert explained all this to me. He was an expert physical therapist who came off as a rambunctious Tibetan monk.

He taught me that if I wanted to be able to wear prostheses, stand up, and walk again one day, I would have to develop my hamstrings and glutes—my ass, basically. But even before that, if I wanted to get around in my wheelchair without screaming in pain at the end of the day (and without developing the bulging physique of a bodybuilder), I'd have to learn to spare my pectoral muscles and rely on my deltoids, instead. Gilbert put me to work, session after session. I hated him. I despised him. I yelled at him. And the more I complained, the more complicated he made the exercises. He was a real sadist, a torturer, even, when he started in on my quadratus lumborum and my iliocostalis. I owe it to him that I can sit up straight. My legs haven't grown back, alas—I'm not a salamander. But I can carry myself proudly, my torso is incredibly flexible, and my slender arms have become more muscular. Thanks to Gilbert, I can now go all over the city *and prove Deepak right: I don't need anyone's help to get around as I like. Except when the elevators in the subway are out of order. Then a little bit of help is welcome.*

13

Ever since she had run into her seventh-floor neighbor in the aisles of their local gourmet food shop the night before, Mrs. Zeldoff had been on a crusade. The conversation had taken place in the fruit and vegetable aisle. Mrs. Williams was buying organic zucchini, the first of the season, when she shared her suspicions with her easy prey.

"Mr. Groomlat thinks the equipment was vandalized?" Mrs. Zeldoff asked in shock.

"He did not dismiss the possibility that someone purposefully let this happen," Mrs. Williams said carefully.

After thinking for a moment and hastening to pick out some of the lovely zucchini for herself, Mrs. Zeldoff added, "Of course, our two elevator operators had everything to gain. If they'd gotten wind of Mr. Groomlat's plan two years ago when he ordered the kit, they could have taken drastic measures."

"As you know, they had every opportunity to do as they pleased," added Mrs. Williams.

"You're completely right—who else had access to that jumble of stuff down there?"

"And according to our dear accountant, they put the equipment in a damp place, as if by chance!"

"Mr. Groomlat told you that?" Mrs. Zeldoff gasped. "May the Lord protect us!"

"You didn't see his e-mail? Would you go and put valuable things in a damp place?"

"Of course not!" exclaimed Mrs. Zeldoff with her hands on her hips. "I'm not an idiot!"

"You're the only person I've told about this," Mrs. Williams whispered in her neighbor's ear.

Mrs. Zeldoff perked up, honored by this sign of trust.

"But perhaps it would be more honest to tell our neighbors about it—after all, they have the right to know what happened, don't you think?" Mrs. Williams added.

This was a real dilemma for Mrs. Zeldoff. She clutched her chin, her eyes darting about the store, wondering what her pastor would tell her to do.

"If you say so . . . ," she ventured.

"I wouldn't want people to accuse me of scheming, especially not the Bronsteins," Mrs. Williams said, adding that she knew from a reliable source that the professor was a left-winger. Didn't they always side with the help?

With every nasty remark, Mrs. Williams tugged at her marionette's invisible strings. Mrs. Zeldoff was so easy to manipulate.

"You should buy these radishes, they're splendid," Mrs. Williams suggested, giddy with delight.

"We could share the task," Mrs. Zeldoff suggested, putting a bunch of the flaming-red roots into her basket.

"That's a very good idea," Mrs. Williams exclaimed. "I'll write to the Hayakawas, and you can spread the good word to the others."

Mrs. Zeldoff had gone home that evening as elated as when someone had told her she had a celestial singing voice one Sunday after her choir performance.

The next morning, she displayed remarkable self-sacrifice and went to knock on Mr. Morrison's door. He was still in his bathrobe, even though it was past eleven o'clock. That was the least of her problems! He didn't understand the first thing about anything.

"Why would our elevator operators sabotage the elevator? They need it to do their job—plus, it works very well. Deepak came up here a little while ago and woke me up . . . for good reason," added the drunken idiot.

"Not the elevator, only the buttons!" she patiently replied.

"What did they do to the buttons? No one touched mine—I just used it yesterday."

"Not those buttons, the other ones," Mrs. Zeldoff said with a groan.

"We have other buttons?"

"Yes, in the basement, if I've understood correctly."

"I didn't know we had buttons in the basement," he muttered. "What are they for?"

"They're not for anything—they were in boxes, so that we could use the elevator without the operators someday."

"What you're telling me is completely ridiculous. We're expected to go to the basement to make the elevator run without Deepak or Mr. Rivera? Excuse me, but if that's the case, then they did a good thing by getting rid of those useless buttons! It's certainly more practical to call the elevator from the landing. What point is there in going down on foot to send the elevator up? Whoever heard of such a thing?"

Mrs. Zeldoff, on the verge of despair, went to continue her crusade three floors up, using the service stairs once again.

Mrs. Clerc seemed very busy. She didn't even offer her a cup of tea. (And they say the French have such good manners!) She only half listened to her and seemed to lend little credence to what she was saying. It truly became annoying—almost unbearable, in fact!—when she became rather vulgar.

"*Madame Williams doit bien se faire chier pour avoir des idées aussi tordues!* Mrs. Williams must really be . . . 'ow do you say . . . bored shitless to come up with such twisted ideas. Deepak is incapable of doing such a sing. I do not know anyone as obsessively clean as 'ee is. 'Ee spends his time polishing everything in ze building—I am afraid even to lean against ze inside of ze elevator."

"Maybe he's not the one, but Mr. Rivera, at night—"

"Okay, eet is very nice to come and tell me all zis, and your theory is captivating, but I 'ave work to do."

"Will you talk to your husband about it?" begged Mrs. Zeldoff.

"I certainly will—I am sure 'ee will be as fascinated as I am. Tell your 'usband 'ello for me," she said, dismissing her.

The nerve! The way she practically kicked her out! Mrs. Zeldoff was not the kind of woman to be treated this way. She marched toward the service door.

"You do not want to use ze front door? Ze elevator is working during ze day," Mrs. Clerc said with surprise.

"A little exercise will do me good," her miffed neighbor replied.

And with some apprehensiveness, she climbed to the ninth floor. Chloe was getting ready to go out and wondered who could be ringing at the service door. This time, to reach the latch, she engaged in some dangerous acrobatics, carefully raising herself up on one arm with her shoulder pressed against the wall.

"Stupid, unfounded, and ludicrous" was the response from Mrs. Zeldoff's young neighbor. Eight flights on foot only to be greeted this way! As if Deepak were a saint! Vaunting his integrity after what he had done was certainly the icing on the cake. And Chloe didn't stop there.

"What you're doing is repulsive. Spreading a rumor always has consequences, so show me some proof or stop your gossiping."

Mrs. Williams was right, Mrs. Zeldoff had concluded. Real left-wing radicals! Being in a wheelchair was no excuse for such rudeness.

Since this impertinent young woman had attacked her integrity, she would call good old Mr. Groomlat and ask him to open an investigation.

She completed her mission before noon, and went home having accomplished her assignment.

◆ ◆ ◆

Deepak got to work early. He expected to be welcomed as a savior, but all morning long, he received nothing but scornful expressions and disapproving looks. Mrs. Clerc barely said hello to him, and Mr. Williams left the building without saying goodbye. Mr. Zeldoff scowled at him and let out a hostile grunt. A little later, his wife rolled her eyes angrily. When Mr. Morrison called for the elevator in midafternoon (he was going out for breakfast) and Deepak asked him why everyone was being so cold, he answered evasively: "Let's talk about it later."

Talk about what? What had gotten into them? Was Mr. Groomlat playing another trick by exaggerating his demands? Had he been let go after all? He could have cashed his check, taken a well-earned retirement, and left them in a fine mess. One year's salary wouldn't bankrupt them: Mrs. Zeldoff wore the equivalent amount in jewelry around her neck; Mrs. Clerc's weekly visits to the hairdresser equaled a week of his pay; every night, Mr. Morrison blew as much money as Deepak earned in a day; and the Williamses were regular gala hoppers, spending the equivalent of a month of Deepak's salary on one marvelous evening just so they could show off in front of the right people. They were all arrogant, ungrateful cheapskates, except for the Bronsteins, who were always very respectful, and Mrs. Collins, who had lost her fortune and her arrogance with it. By noon, Deepak still hadn't calmed down. Lali was right—he was a sucker. If he were a mean bastard like the concierge at 16 5th Avenue, they would all be eating out of his hand. Maybe he should go see the accountant and tell him that, after thinking it over, he had decided to stick with the original plan. They could just pay him his due and get by without him.

At three p.m., Deepak was still brooding behind his desk. He had sent the dog walker packing after the Clercs' golden retriever had come back from the park in a wretched state. "Who's going to clean the marble in the lobby?" he had shouted at him. The dog walker had left dumbfounded.

Next, the liquor store delivered a case of wine for Mr. Morrison. Who was going to put the bottles away in the sideboard in his living room? Then the florist showed up with a bouquet for Mrs. Williams that was so sumptuous it wouldn't fit into the elevator without scattering petals all over the place. Who was going to sweep up?

But when Chloe appeared at four in a more pitiful state than the Clercs' dog, Deepak became himself again.

"What happened to you?" he asked.

"Nothing," she replied calmly. "The elevator at the subway station was broken again, so I had to get off at the next station, and it's ten blocks from here. Using your arms, it's quite a hike . . . so to speak. I'm wiped out."

"Why didn't you take the bus?" he asked as he pushed her toward the elevator.

"Because it takes forever to lower the ramp, and people get impatient. Plus, the buses are packed at this time of day, so I always end up stuck in front of the door, near the driver. At every stop, people bump into me getting on and off. And in a wheelchair, the sudden stops give you terrible nausea. The subway elevators, when they exist, are unpredictable. Most of the time, nice people help me get upstairs, but that didn't happen today. Okay, I've complained enough, we should be celebrating that you're staying."

"How do you know?" Deepak asked between the fifth and sixth floors. "I only found out around ten a.m., and you were still at home—I brought you down around noon."

Deepak opened the gate, moved out of the way so Chloe could pass, and went back down without getting any answer.

On the way, he stopped at the second floor and rang Mr. Groomlat's bell.

The accountant was waiting for him behind his desk. He handed him his contract. Deepak stuck it in his pocket.

"Aren't you going to read it?"

"I trust you, and since everyone is giving me the cold shoulder today, I certainly understand that my demands weren't very popular."

"Sit down a moment," said the accountant. Deepak remained standing.

"As you like. Since you trust me, I'm going to return the favor. They still don't know about your demands. I just told them I rehired you. Don't worry, I have the authority to act in the interest of the co-op. I'm sure they'll be relieved not to have to pay the additional charges I had requested. Nevertheless, I'd prefer that our little agreement remains between us. By the time you leave, it'll be water under the bridge. By the way, why eighteen months? You could've rounded up to two years," Groomlat asked.

"You wouldn't understand," Deepak replied as he left.

◆ ◆ ◆

When his shift was over, Deepak visited Mr. Rivera in the hospital. Mrs. Collins hadn't sent a book with him this time, since she had brought one over herself in the middle of the afternoon. She was also the only person who still greeted Deepak normally. The residents' behavior continued to bother him.

Mr. Rivera, who had seen him so cheerful the day before, was worried to find him in such a gloomy mood now.

"You seem very troubled."

"I don't understand what's going on. They've never been so horrible—well, never all at once. It's like they're holding something against me."

"Like what? The fact that you swallowed your pride and agreed to keep working there? That would be a messed-up state of affairs."

"So why are they all being so rude to me?"

"If you want my opinion, they must have been glad to be done with us and see their expenses decrease. They're disappointed, that's all. Did you tell them about your nephew?"

"Not yet—I'll do it on Monday. I'm meeting a guy from the union tomorrow for coffee."

"On Saturday? I'm impressed."

"I'd rather make my case outside their office. What I'm asking him to do isn't very legal."

"You really think of everything."

"Only what's necessary."

"They're just worried about the night shift. When they find out it's been taken care of, everything will go back to normal."

"Even Mr. Morrison wasn't acting like himself," Deepak fretted.

"I've never seen him when he wasn't soused. Maybe he indulged too much the night before. We should just be grateful things worked out this way—it's a real lifesaver."

Deepak left his colleague at nine. In the subway on his way home, he asked himself whether this lifesaver had a name.

◆ ◆ ◆

When he got home, he found Lali at the table with Sanji and was sure, as he took off his jacket, that the room had fallen silent the moment he'd arrived.

"I waited for you today," Deepak said as he sat down.

"I finished up later than expected," Sanji replied nonchalantly.

"You could've let me know."

Lali flew to her nephew's rescue.

"Sanji was in a meeting with important people."

"So I'm not important? You start Monday," he continued.

"Did you go see the union people?" Lali asked as she placed the dish on the table.

"It'll happen tomorrow," Deepak replied, scooping a helping of food onto his wife's plate.

"Do you work every day?" Sanji asked.

"Why do you ask?"

"What do they do when you go on vacation?"

"We get a replacement," Deepak said. "But he's only available on weekends and in August. Mr. Rivera has Saturdays off, and I have Sundays; we switched this time so I could meet with the union tomorrow. In the summer, we each take two weeks at different times. That way there's always someone to replace us, either during the day or at night."

"And this replacement wasn't available?"

"If he were, we would have solved this problem a long time ago. But if you've changed your mind, go ahead and tell me. Things can't get much worse!"

"What's wrong?" Lali asked in a worried voice.

"What could possibly be wrong? Luck is on our side—the equipment that should have ended my career was miraculously damaged. And tomorrow I'll lie to my oldest friends by claiming my nephew by marriage is an experienced elevator operator from Mumbai, although I still have no idea what he does for a living. I'm just wondering if when I shave tomorrow morning, I'll still recognize myself in the mirror."

◆ ◆ ◆

Just before midnight, Deepak put on his pajamas, slipped into bed, and turned off his bedside lamp. Lali turned hers back on.

"Do you want to tell me what's bothering you or would you prefer that I spend all night worrying about it by myself?"

"Why did you go see Miss Chloe?" Deepak said.

"Some traditions never die. For an old Indian man like you, two women talking must be up to something."

"This old Indian man gave up his career to marry an old Indian woman like you! Anyway, I know you, and when you overreact, it's because you have something on your conscience."

"And what exactly am I feeling so guilty about? I'm dying to know."

"There's not an ounce of humidity in my storeroom. Do you think I'd leave my uniform there if it were damp? So what do you think it was that corroded their equipment?"

"I'm a specialist in electronics now, I suppose?"

"No, but isn't that your nephew's area?"

"How silly of me, it's a conspiracy! Your wife, your nephew, your protégée on the ninth floor—everyone's in league to commit sabotage with the single purpose of saving your job and your absurd aspirations. Oh, I almost forgot poor Mr. Rivera, who sent me a map of the basement by carrier pigeon to show me the location of some equipment I wouldn't recognize even if I were looking for it. And then I must have left in the middle of the night while you were sleeping, crept into the basement, and peed on it!"

"Don't be ridiculous—I didn't accuse you of anything."

"And I'm supposed to be the one with something on my conscience! You should hear yourself," Lali fumed.

"You always have an answer for everything, but I can't help but think that something funny is going on here. And if I come under the least bit of suspicion, I know someone who will jump at the chance to make me pay."

14

Lali and Sanji were at the breakfast table. Deepak came out of his room wearing wide white pants and a matching polo shirt. Sanji had never seen him looking so chic.

"I thought you were going to have coffee with your colleagues from the union?" Lali asked in surprise.

"My athletic background always impresses them. Plus, I'm going to go throw a few balls in the park when I'm done."

"You should go with your uncle—he has a veritable fan club there," Lali suggested to her nephew.

"I'd love to see him play," Sanji replied, looking at his cell phone, "but I have an unexpected business lunch."

"On Saturday?" Deepak exclaimed.

"You have a work meeting, so why shouldn't he?" Lali interjected.

"If I said it was going to rain, your aunt would rush to tell me that it wasn't your fault."

"You can go another time," she added, ignoring her husband's comment. "Try not to work tomorrow—I'd like for us to spend a little time together."

Sanji promised and went to get ready.

"And what about you—are you coming to see me play?" Deepak asked his wife coyly.

"I wouldn't miss it for the world, just like every weekend since we met. I'll see you on the field around noon."

◆ ◆ ◆

At noon, Sanji met Sam at Claudette's. The restaurant was near his office, and Sam loved their brunch menu.

"What's so urgent?" Sanji asked as he sat down.

"I've got the paperwork for your American branch. Here, sign these forms. I'll drop them off on Monday. All we need now is your contribution, and that won't be a problem, right?"

While Sam was talking, Sanji had turned to look at two people just entering the restaurant.

"Are you listening?" Sam tried to get Sanji's attention. "Stop, you shouldn't do that!"

"What shouldn't I do?"

"Stare at a woman like her."

"A woman like her?"

"In a wheelchair!"

"I know her," Sanji replied nonchalantly, turning back toward Sam. "What were you saying?"

"You're kidding, right?"

"Don't worry, my banker didn't call me back, but I'll get hold of him this afternoon, and everything will be taken care of this week."

"I don't care about your banker, I was talking about that woman. You really know her?"

Sanji didn't answer. Out of the corner of his eye, he was watching the owner welcoming his guests the way people of the highest castes were treated back home. She said she had been an actress—was she a star? Yet the owner was the only one paying attention to her. In Mumbai, everyone would have rushed over to ask for an autograph, or even a selfie. In any case, *she* was the one he was staring at, not her wheelchair. And maybe also at the man sitting across from her.

"This time, you're the one looking at another table. Do you know those guys?"

"Not really—well, I know one of them a little bit."

"Which one?" the professor asked.

"The one sitting by the wall," Chloe replied, grabbing the menu.

"Where did you meet him?"

"We exchanged a few words in the park. His father was a musician. I'm thinking of eggs Benedict. What about you?"

"He seems nice."

"Or maybe scrambled eggs?"

"What does he do for a living?" Mr. Bronstein persisted.

"He's one of the genius entrepreneurs of the modern world. He came to find investors in New York."

"A genius? That's strong praise!"

"Well, just brilliant, maybe. Should we order? I'm starving."

"Brilliant in what way?"

"All right, cut it out, what are you implying?"

"Nothing. It's just strange that you're studying a menu you know by heart. I haven't seen you blush like this in a long time."

"I'm not blushing."

"Look at yourself in the mirror above my head."

"I'm hot, that's all."

"With the AC on full blast?"

"Okay, can we please change the subject?"

"How's our philosopher?" Mr. Bronstein asked innocently.

"I'll find out when we have a night elevator operator," she snapped.

"I've been invited to give a lecture next week," he continued. "A banking conference, and the pay is pretty good."

"Don't look so down—that's good news," Chloe said cheerfully. "The Bronsteins have wind in their sails. I just signed on to do another recording. Now that this whole business of extra charges won't be happening, the two of us should be able to pay off our debts pretty soon."

"Maybe even redo the plumbing in your bathroom."

"Should we drink to the faucets, then?" Chloe asked brightly.

"No, let's drink to your career!"

"And to your lecture series!"

"I'll have to go to San Francisco. So I'll be away for a few days. Will you be able to manage—"

"To get by without you? I do it every day. Plus, I can always count on Deepak if there's a problem."

"Should we ask them to join us?" asked the professor with a twinkle in his eye, looking at the two men sitting across from him.

"Keep your voice down!"

◆ ◆ ◆

Sanji paid the bill. Sam pulled the table toward him so Sanji could get out. Chloe watched their movements in the mirror above her father. Sanji turned back just before leaving the restaurant, and as their eyes met briefly, Chloe looked down at her plate—her father couldn't help but notice.

◆ ◆ ◆

Sam had a date and said goodbye to Sanji in front of the fence around Washington Square Park. Sanji wandered around the fountain. Watching people and imagining their lives was one of his favorite pastimes. Maybe that was even what had made him design his app. In his youth, he was fascinated by the absurdity of life in big cities, where so many people lived side by side without ever speaking to each other. The loneliness of his childhood also had something to do with it. When he had begun his career as an entrepreneur, his uncles had accused him of dishonoring the family. Men and women were only supposed to meet with the agreement of their families and could only spend time together once their match had been approved. Sanji belonged to a generation that didn't see life that way. But breaking taboos, shedding traditions, winning one's freedom, and learning how to use it were not fights that could be won in a single day. Although he didn't know much about them, he admired the courage Lali and Deepak had shown by leaving everything behind.

He thought again of how easily Chloe had approached him in the park that day; he probably would never have dared speak to her. His ringtone interrupted his thoughts. It was a call from the Mumbai Palace Hotel.

Taresh and Vikram, his uncles, told him that they had prevented him from using his shares as security. A clause in the hotel's articles of incorporation allowed them to. They were revolted by his irresponsible behavior.

"If you fail," Taresh argued, "one-third of our palace will fall into foreign hands, you scoundrel!"

"How can you be so selfish as to risk our life's work and put your family's legacy in danger? And for what?" Vikram railed at him.

"What family are you talking about?" Sanji replied before hanging up on them.

His uncles wanted war. Furious, he left the fountain to go to another park in the city, where an uncle worthy of the title was playing cricket.

◆ ◆ ◆

Chloe entered Washington Square Park and went to sit at one of the tables where seasoned chess players took cocky amateurs to the cleaners. She didn't spend her Saturday afternoons this way for the handful of bills she pocketed after every game, but for the pleasure of winning. She had been a driven athlete and sometimes regretted getting rid of all her trophies. Her last competition had taken place five years ago, one morning in April.

◆ ◆ ◆

Sanji admired the elegant way Deepak handled his bat. Deepak was surrounded by a flock of teenagers from the northern neighborhoods of the city who dreamed of becoming champions.

"I understand why you fell for him when you saw him in Shivaji Park," Sanji said.

"He's much more handsome now," Lali replied. "For some people, Deepak is just an elevator operator, but on the cricket field, he's a true king."

"It must not have been easy to leave."

"Leaving was the easiest part. One night, when Deepak went out, three thugs jumped him and beat him up. We knew who was behind it, and we got the message my parents were sending us. When I went to visit him in the clinic, he did everything he could to try to end our relationship. He said his love for me would last forever but that we couldn't plan a future together. He claimed he didn't have the right to sully the reputation of a family like ours, much less the right to ruin my life. I blamed his momentary confusion on his injuries, and told him this would be the last time I would tolerate someone trying to take control of my life, which I had decided to spend by his side. I would leave home with no regrets. My family didn't exist anymore—I had nothing in common with people who were capable of such violence. For months, day after day, I stashed my things into a bundle of dirty laundry buried in the back of a wardrobe so that our servants wouldn't notice anything. Under my bed, I hid the small amount of money that I had managed to pilfer from my mother's purse and from the pockets of my father's pants that he left lying around. I stole from my brothers as well. Deepak came to get me in the middle of the night. He was waiting for me near our house and had told me he would understand if I didn't show up. I slipped out of the house quietly. You can't imagine how scared I was as I crept through the hallway while everyone was asleep, then went downstairs and closed the door behind me, never to return. I still have dreams about it sometimes, and I wake up trembling. We fled on foot, and it was a race against time, because we had to get to the port before sunrise. A rickshaw driver took pity on us and agreed to take us. Deepak had paid a fortune for two berths on a cargo ship. We spent forty-two days at sea. I lent a hand in the kitchen, and Deepak helped the crew—he got stuck with the worst jobs. But what a journey! The Arabian Sea, the Red Sea, the Suez Canal, the Mediterranean, the Strait of Gibraltar . . . and finally, we truly embraced our freedom."

"Why only then, since you'd been at sea for a while?"

"Because it was on a night in Gibraltar, where the ship stopped, that we made love for the first time. But, as I said, this was the easiest part of our escape. I refused to be an illegal immigrant, and Deepak loved rules too much to endure living here illegally very long. I won't deny that his excessive honesty has sometimes gotten on my nerves. We went to the immigration office. At that time, the people who governed this nation of immigrants still remembered their ancestors' stories and where they came from. The fact that our lives had been threatened allowed us to obtain refugee status, and Deepak's scars were evidence that we were telling the truth. We were given temporary papers and, to our great surprise, a bit of money to take care of our needs and start a new life. Deepak didn't want to take it." Lali laughed heartily. "I took it for him."

"And then?" Sanji asked.

Lali was silent. He noticed that she seemed upset and put his arm around her shoulder.

"I'm sorry," he said. "I don't want to stir up painful memories."

"I lied to you," Lali continued in a low voice. "It's not true that I didn't lose anything when I left my family's home. Because I left part of myself there, and despite my pride—which has led me astray a few times—I suffered from it terribly, and I still suffer from it. I once had a privileged, carefree life, and suddenly I found myself moving from one menial job to the next, working up to sixteen hours a day so we wouldn't go hungry. It was bloody difficult, and while we can't complain, what we have after all these years is only just enough for us to get by in our old age, provided we don't live too long. If Deepak had to retire now, I don't know how we could make ends meet. Okay, enough questions. Tell me about my family and the country that I hate for what it put me through, but still miss desperately."

Sanji told her about that country, that it was the biggest democracy in the world, that it still struggled with poverty and a social order maintained by a caste system. But not everything was so dire. Beyond the stereotypical images of India—the sacred cows, the slums, Bollywood, and the generation of computer engineers that he belonged to—there was progress, the cities were modernizing, poverty was decreasing, the country had a free press, and a middle class was emerging.

Lali interrupted him.

"I'm not asking you for a lesson in economics or geopolitics. I can get that from my husband who bores me to death reading his newspaper out loud. Tell me about you, tell me what you care about. Do you have a fiancée?"

Sanji took a deep breath before answering her. He turned toward her slowly and looked her straight in the eye.

"Aunt Lali, the old, decrepit buildings that your father owned have become a great palace, the most luxurious one in Mumbai. Your brothers hid that from you."

Lali held her breath and looked at him, speechless.

"Why did you bother to come see me play if you chatterboxes are just going to stand there jabbering away?" Deepak groused as he strode over to them. "I hope this conversation was worth missing my splendid throw!"

The Day I Hit Julius

The day started with physical therapy. That bastard Gilbert was having a field day. It wasn't a typical morning, because I was going to take my first steps with my prostheses. I fell down, but that's not why everything went to hell. The pain probably played a role, but it was something else.

Before 2:50, Dad traveled a lot, and I spent a lot of time alone at 12 5th Avenue. Julius's studio is a real turnoff: the yellow stucco walls, the old carpet smell, and the ghastly light from the ceiling fixture make it the least romantic place in the world. Julius isn't very good at interior design. Plus, the walls are very thin, and the noises from the neighboring apartments make it feel haunted. Plenty of reason for us to make love at my place whenever my dad wasn't there. But Dad wasn't traveling anymore.

Luckily, he taught in the afternoons.

Julius took me in his arms, laid me down on the bed, and kissed me. He lay on top of me and unbuttoned my dress. When he caressed my breasts, it was the first time I had felt his desire since 2:50. His lips glided across my skin and down to my belly, but when he began to spread my legs apart I saw his face freeze. I slapped him.

We don't make love anymore.

15

Chloe spent a long time in front of her closet before choosing a long gingham skirt and a white scoop-neck blouse.

In the early afternoon, Deepak had rung her doorbell to tell her the news. A replacement who met Mr. Groomlat's requirements had just been hired. The new nighttime operator, experienced and union certified, would begin work at 7:15 p.m. "Well, fairly experienced," he added in his typical truthful fashion. Chloe was free to come and go as she pleased once again.

If she could have gotten up, she would have hugged him. Deepak must have realized this, because she saw him almost blush. He stepped back into the elevator with a funny bow that confirmed their mutual excitement.

Since her father was in San Francisco, she suggested to Julius that they go out to dinner. The call went straight to voice mail, so she left him a message with the address of the restaurant where they were to meet at eight.

She checked her makeup one last time in the mirror, and went through the apartment turning off all the lights except the table lamp in the foyer. Then she picked up her cell phone and called the elevator.

While the elevator was on its way up, she turned herself around on the landing. The new operator slid open the gate and flattened himself against the handle as Chloe rolled in backward.

She could only see his back. Mr. Rivera's uniform was too big for him: the shoulders extended sloppily over his arms, and the sleeves of the coat partially covered his hands.

"Good evening, miss," he said in a deferential tone.

"Good evening, it's so wonderful to have you . . ."

She interrupted herself in the middle of her sentence, looking more intently at the back of the operator's neck.

"You were saying?" the operator said at the seventh floor.

Chloe felt her heart beating a mile a minute as they went past the fifth floor.

"That it would be good manners to turn around and look at the person who's speaking to you."

Sanji did so.

"So I guess this is your way of telling me that you lied to me."

"I didn't lie to you."

"Entrepreneur? Indian Facebook? My ass!"

"It's a luxury to have only one job in New York—didn't you say that yourself?" Sanji replied.

"And on the weekends, you're a Bollywood star or a champion paraglider, I suppose?"

"I'm afraid of heights, and a very bad actor."

"Could've fooled me!"

The elevator came to an abrupt halt four inches above the ground floor.

"I still haven't totally mastered it. I'll take us back up to the second floor—you deserve a better landing."

"It just gets better and better . . ."

"I'm doing my best, and you could be a little more patient."

"You didn't have a meeting at 28th Street. I saw the cab turn around. It seems you lie all the time."

"Here we go, we're almost level this time, miss. You should be able to get out without any problem. I was advised not to touch your wheelchair. But I will escort you to the sidewalk and hail you a cab, miss."

"Stop it with this 'miss' stuff!" Chloe snapped. "And don't you accompany me anywhere," she said over her shoulder as she passed the desk, where, to her surprise, she saw Deepak.

"An elevator operator isn't good enough for you, is that it?" Sanji shouted in reply.

Deepak hurried to open the door for Chloe and watched as she crossed the street toward Claudette's.

"What have I done now?" Sanji asked, irritated, when Deepak returned.

"I stayed to make sure you were doing okay. You have just three rules, three tiny little rules. Let me repeat them: be courteous; be invisible if no one addresses you; and if someone does speak, listen to the questions you're asked but never answer them. Is that so difficult?"

"She didn't ask me a question, she started a conversation!"

"Not 'she'—'Miss Chloe.' As you passed the fourth floor, I could already hear you raising your voice. And I'm not even going to mention how you stopped the elevator. I'm grateful for what you're doing for me, but if you don't do the job well, it's not worth the effort. I'm going to see Rivera now, and then go home to bed. I'm entrusting you with my building. I hope to find it in perfect condition tomorrow. Can I count on you? And don't forget to help Mr. Morrison get into his apartment."

Sanji gritted his teeth as his uncle went downstairs to change in the storeroom.

◆ ◆ ◆

Chloe came home alone at ten. She didn't say a word to Sanji in the elevator, just a begrudging "good night" when she reached her floor.

Without turning on the lights, she rolled her wheelchair over to the window. It was Monday, and the streets were empty, except for a few taxis that sped down 5th Avenue and turned onto 9th Street. Chloe stayed there for a long time, staring into space. Around midnight, she put her hand in her pocket and pressed the button to speed-dial Julius. She had made up her mind. It wasn't because he had stood her up—he must have had to work late and might not have even gotten her message.

While she had waited for him, Claude had offered her a glass of champagne, then another, and then a third. Before she got really drunk, though her mind was already a bit cloudy, he had sat down across from her and ordered dinner for the two of them. The owner of Claudette's had taken pity on her, and pity was something that Chloe could no longer stand, not from Julius or from anyone else.

She didn't want to hear his voice. With her cell phone in hand, she waited for the automated greeting to finish, and then she left a message.

"I've been wrong so many times, it's pathetic. I was wrong about how much I could put up with while we pretended to still be together. I was wrong about the way I should put my life back together and wrong about what I hoped to get out of our relationship. I was wrong to feel like I owed you something—I was wrong about us and especially about me. But that's it, I don't want to be wrong anymore, ever. Meet me in the park tomorrow. I know you don't have class between three and four. I'll give you back the few things you left here and, along with them, your freedom. I'm taking mine back. Goodbye, Schopenhauer."

◆ ◆ ◆

The next day, Chloe entered Washington Square Park at three p.m. As she came down the path, she saw someone other than Julius seated on the bench.

"What are you doing here?" she asked.

"He won't come," Sanji said with a sigh, closing his book.

"I don't understand."

"Last night when you called, I didn't have the heart to tell you that you'd dialed the wrong number."

16

"Why did you stay with this man if you were wrong about everything?" Sanji asked.

"Because he stayed with me, and because I had gone through so much physically that I didn't want to risk any other kind of suffering."

"Is his name really Schopenhauer?"

"Unless he's changed it since yesterday."

"It's pretty brave to fall in love with a guy with a name like that. Or maybe just extremely masochistic."

"What does his name have to do with how I may or may not feel about him?"

"Schopenhauer's essay on women is even more misogynistic than the misogyny embedded in my country's collective unconscious."

"I was with the copy, not the original. You've actually read Schopenhauer?"

"Does that surprise you because I'm from Mumbai? I don't blame you—I'm always pleasantly surprised whenever a Westerner's view of India extends beyond an image of sacred cows and mango chutney."

"That's not what I meant."

"But you implied it."

"You're a fine one to be lecturing me. Which one of us is a barefaced liar, after all?"

"If I had told you my appointment was in the opposite direction from yours, you would have felt like you owed me something. And as I think I learned from the message you left last night, you don't like to feel that way."

"You know very well I wasn't thinking about that, and by the way, if you ever hope to speak to me again, let's agree that that phone call never happened."

"Okay, and then you can tell me which of us is the bigger liar. But never mind that, what matters is that you agree to see me again, even though you know I'm just a lowly elevator operator."

"It would be hard not to see you again, now that you work in my building."

"Oh, I would hate for you to feel obliged to see me. I'll go back to calling you 'miss,' and you'll only hear from me if you need my services. Sorry about the wrong number . . . I won't mention it again, I promise."

"Chloe, not 'miss'!" she called after Sanji as he left.

And she watched him until he turned a corner and disappeared from sight.

◆ ◆ ◆

Deepak looked at his watch, hoping Sanji would be on time. His wish was granted, give or take five minutes.

"I did my best," his nephew protested breathlessly.

"I wasn't going to say anything. After midnight, and only after making sure that everyone was home, of course, Rivera would usually get some rest behind the desk. But set an alarm so you can be present- able starting at six thirty. Sometimes Mr. Williams goes out to buy the newspaper around six forty-five. Don't worry, your nights will be less tiring than my days."

"Except that I work during the daytime, too."

"Rivera spends his days visiting his wife in the nursing home, and believe me, judging by his state afterward, it's not at all restful. He's forty years older than you, so you should be able to manage."

"Would it hurt to say 'thank you'?"

"You should know that some silences speak louder than unnecessary words. See you tomorrow. I leave the place in your hands."

Deepak went down to the basement. Rivera had been mistaken in thinking that the owners' behavior would go back to normal as soon as his replacement had started. Their unusual unfriendliness troubled him more and more. Mrs. Williams, an expert in cutting remarks, had casually tossed one off to him as she left the elevator. "It's a miracle, as Mrs. Zeldoff would be quick to point out. Finding an elevator operator at the last minute is nothing short of astounding. And what a coincidence, he's from India! I guess there aren't any qualified workers in America anymore?"

Deepak's instincts had rarely been wrong, and he decided to get to the bottom of this. After putting away his uniform, he went to the little area across from the storeroom where a VCR recorded the surveillance camera footage between eleven p.m. and seven a.m. One camera was aimed at the sidewalk under the awning, the second displayed the service entrance, and the third was in the basement hallway. Ever since the surveillance equipment had been installed twenty years ago, nothing significant had happened. The co-op kept a set of six old VHS cassettes that Deepak rotated.

He sat in front of the monitor, inserted the first one, and fast-forwarded it. As he watched the tape from the previous Wednesday, he was stupefied to see Mrs. Collins enter his storeroom in her dressing gown, armed with a spray bottle. He had no idea what substance it contained, but you didn't have to be a private eye to figure out what it had been used for. This evidence was enough to clear his name, but after thinking about it for a few minutes, Deepak rewound the cassette and left it in the machine. That night's recording would erase all traces of this unexpected visit, and he would remain the only witness.

Deepak left shortly afterward. It was too late to go see Rivera, so he went straight home.

◆ ◆ ◆

Mr. Morrison had gotten home safe and sound. Following Deepak's advice, Sanji had not said anything more than a simple hello.

It was soon midnight, and he let out a big yawn. He put his feet up on the desk and leaned back in the chair. As it proved impossible to fall asleep, Sanji brainstormed ways to kill time. He found a notepad and a pencil that he chewed on for quite a while as he chose his words.

At one a.m., he went up to the ninth floor, stepped over the three-inch gap between the elevator and the landing, and slid a folded piece of paper under the door. He went back down and dozed off around three a.m., lying in the middle of the lobby with his arms outstretched.

The Day I Smelled the Roses

Dad came back in the early afternoon with no explanation. I was at the living room window. Whenever he asks me why I spend so much time with my face pressed to the glass, I reply that looking at the street is good for me. This is a total mystery to him. The real reason is because that's where I like to write, and I look out at the street each time I need to take a break. And every time he finds me there, I hide my notebook. Why not tell him I keep a journal? Because a journal is a secret garden, that's why. But that day, Dad was upset with me for staying indoors. "I want you to go get some air—in fact, I don't want to see you back here for at least two hours!"

I stared at him in astonishment. Even when I was a teenager, he never ordered me to do anything. Why was it suddenly so important for me to clear out? I casually asked if he had a girlfriend. Then he was the one who looked surprised—he didn't see the connection! I wasn't going to spell it out for him.

Since I'd been kicked out, I wheeled my way through the park. First I went around the fountain, and then I went over to the bench where I used to sit and listen to a trumpet player who played almost every afternoon. Sometimes, to win over his listeners, he even played two trumpets at once. A real virtuoso!

It was late spring, and the roses were in bloom. Floribunda, Gentle Hermione, The Pilgrim, James Galway, Queen of Sweden: I could smell every variety. I was alive.

When I got back home, I thanked my father and asked him again if he had a girlfriend. Before he could answer, I left and went to sit by the window in my room.

17

"Seriously? This is too much," Sam griped.

"What? I'm right on time!" said Sanji, dropping his bag onto Sam's desk.

"To start with, you could've changed. You're wearing the same clothes as yesterday, and you haven't shaved."

"Sorry, didn't have time," Sanji replied with a big yawn.

"That's not all!"

"What now?"

"Did you join the Queen's Guard? What's with the ridiculous hat?"

Sanji looked up and realized he had forgotten to take off the cap that went with his uniform.

"Okay, I get it. You had a wild night and didn't get home till dawn. I hope it was worth it."

"Let's just say I didn't sleep well, or very much."

"Who with?" taunted Sam, leaning over his desk.

"It's too complicated to explain, and it's not what you think."

"That's what the wife's lover says when the husband finds him hiding in the closet."

"Why do you Americans always think everyone is lying?"

"So I'm right. What's her name?"

"Otis."

"Is that a woman's name?"

"An elevator's."

"Are you all this crazy in Mumbai? You spent the night in an elevator?"

"Something like that, yes."

"You know, if it gets stuck, there's an emergency button."

"Who said it was stuck?"

Sam took an electric razor out of his drawer and handed it to Sanji.

"Go clean yourself up in the bathroom. Our meeting is in fifteen minutes—try to look presentable and take off that hat!"

During the meeting, Sam did his best to highlight the qualities of their project, the amazing profits that could be expected, and the fabulous access to the Indian market. Meanwhile, Sanji yawned continually. And when Sanji slipped him a note under the table, Sam almost choked in the middle of his sentence and wondered seriously if his friend was on something. He put the paper in his pocket and tried to finish his presentation as best he could.

After escorting his clients out, Sam found Sanji lying on his desk with his eyes closed.

"What are you doing?"

"Please, just let me rest a few minutes."

"Was this Otis woman really so amazing? What's the meaning of this message you gave me during the meeting?"

"What did you think of it?"

"It's ridiculous."

"Really?" Sanji asked worriedly, jumping up from the desk.

"'The only unforgivable thing is not to forgive.' Did you come up with that on your own?"

"I think I read it somewhere. It sounds good, and it makes a lot of sense, don't you think?"

"No, but I forgive you anyway. Try to be in better shape tomorrow."

"The message wasn't for you, idiot. You have more experience with women than I do. I wasn't sure, so I wanted your opinion."

"Wasn't sure about what?" Sam asked.

"She hasn't decided yet if she'll agree to speak to me again, so I wrote to her."

"You didn't spend the night outside her apartment, I hope? That would be pathetic. And what did you do to make her so mad?"

"I don't know if it's the lie or my job that bothers her."

"Maybe she just didn't like your hat. What did you lie about?"

"I could've explained it to her, but I didn't want to anymore after seeing her reaction."

"Explain what?" Sam asked, annoyed.

"Haven't you ever dreamed of making a woman like you without projecting or pretending or justifying anything—just by being yourself?"

"No."

"Can I sleep here for a little while? I won't bother you, I promise."

Sam looked at Sanji seriously.

"Look around and tell me if anything in this room makes you think it's a hotel room. No? Well, that's because my office isn't a fun house, and I still have a boss, in case you've forgotten. The day is over—you can just go back home."

"Too bad, I'll find some other way." Sanji sighed.

He left, stumbling from fatigue, as Sam watched in dismay.

He had an hour before his shift started, just enough time to get to Spanish Harlem and freshen up and change, but he would have to see Lali, and having a conversation was more than he could handle. He walked two blocks, entered Washington Square Park, and collapsed onto the first bench he saw.

Sanji heard a quiet whirring noise. He sat up, half opened his eyes, and saw Chloe's wheelchair disappear down a nearby path. He rubbed his face and, putting his hand on his stomach, found a piece of paper that read:

Humor is essential.
I like your idea a lot.

Sanji put the note in his pocket and ran to 5th Avenue. Seeing his reflection in a window, he started to fret about his appearance. Sprawled out on a bench, in his rumpled clothing, he couldn't have been any less attractive. He avoided the lobby, slipped into the service entrance, and, after putting on his uniform, joined Deepak.

"What about your cap?" his uncle asked.

"Sorry, I forgot it."

"Don't tell me, I don't want to know. In the meantime, take mine. It seems that you also forgot to take a shower."

◆ ◆ ◆

The night had been calm. Sanji was waiting for the last of his charges to return. Mr. Morrison staggered into the lobby, then went back out under the awning and started wandering off in the other direction. Sanji came to his rescue as he was about to cross the street.

"Do you like Haydn?" Mr. Morrison asked with a hiccup.

"Don't know him."

"It was horrific. A shitty performance, if you ask me. And the face that bass player made every time he moved his bow was ridiculous. Let's go out. I know a great little bar."

"How about we get you to bed, if that's all right with you."

"Well, young man, I think we have a misunderstanding here. I don't even know you. Who are you anyway?" he questioned as Sanji pulled him along firmly toward the elevator.

"Your nighttime elevator operator."

"I don't know what's going on in this damn building—they told me they were putting in buttons. But no one told me which one I should press."

Sanji closed the gate and turned the handle. As the elevator went up, Mr. Morrison slowly slid down the wall.

"Three sentences—I only said three sentences, not a lullaby," Sanji groaned as he lifted him up.

He put him down on the landing and tried several keys on the key ring that Deepak had given him before finding the right one. Inside the apartment, he wondered which door led to the bedroom. There was no way Mr. Morrison could tell him. The third one was the right one, and he laid him out on the bed. When Mr. Morrison gave a little moan, Sanji took pity on him and removed his shoes. The worn heels of his socks and his big toes poking out of them said much about the stout little man's lonely life. Sanji managed to work off his jacket, adjusted the pillows, covered him with a blanket, and left.

Passing by the bathroom, he hesitated for a moment and decided he should risk it. The shower was revitalizing. He grabbed a clean towel from a shelf and dried himself off.

It was hard to resist the call of the living room couch since his back was aching after a night sleeping on the marble floor of the lobby.

Sanji set the alarm on his cell phone and placed it right next to his ear. Before closing his eyes, he wondered if Chloe would decide to leave the apartment one evening soon. What good was it playing elevator operator if she stayed shut in at home? And what was this idea she liked? He hoped he could ask her soon.

At four a.m., Mr. Morrison's bladder led him to the bathroom. He heard snoring in the living room and he had a vision of an Indian man sleeping on the couch in his underwear. Mr. Morrison blinked twice and told himself that he should probably ease up on the drinking a little.

18

Deepak was intrigued to find his nephew looking fresh and well rested.

"Did you abandon your position last night?"

"Not for a second," Sanji assured him solemnly.

"Then your hair must be like that self-cleaning oven Lali dreams of, and which I hope to give her one day. Never mind. I brought you some clean clothes—it was your aunt's idea," he explained, handing him a bag. "I'll stay later tonight. She asked me to, so you can have a little break. You can come take over for me around eight."

Leaving the building, Sanji looked up toward the top-floor windows. He thought he saw Chloe and waved to her.

She backed away from the window, holding in her hand the little note she had just found under her door.

I don't know what idea you were talking about, but I've had a better one. Meet me at 5:30 in the park, and please don't hesitate to wake me up this time.

Sanji

◆ ◆ ◆

"You have a nice name. I've never heard it before," Chloe said, joining Sanji, who was waiting for her on the bench.

"They'd love yours in Mumbai," he replied, handing her a waffle. "I bought these on the corner—they looked delicious."

"You were so sure I would come?"

"I was sure I could eat two."

"How about going for a walk?" Chloe suggested.

Sanji walked next to her. He was dying to ask her a question and resisted for a minute before asking it.

"What happened between you and this Schopenhauer guy?"

"Are you really interested in my life or are you just asking to be polite?"

"To be polite," Sanji replied.

"Come on, let's go over by the fountain—it's the most cheerful part of the park."

She was right: a clumsy juggler was struggling to catch colorful balls that flew everywhere, a woman was drawing chalk portraits on the ground, two men were kissing on the grass, and children were darting about through the jets of water. Sanji sat on the edge, and Chloe positioned her chair next to him and looked at the pashmina on her lap.

"I wasn't always like this, and something in our relationship disappeared with that part of me."

"Your sense of humor, your quick wit, your eyes, your smile—all that wasn't enough for him?"

"I'd prefer to change the subject."

"I wouldn't."

"It's very nice of you to tell me all this, but since you were the unintended witness of this breakup, I'd like to remind you that *I* broke up with *him*."

"Not exactly."

"What do you mean 'not exactly'?"

"You broke up with *me*. I can't hold it against you since it was a wrong number, but now that I think about it, maybe I would have preferred it not to be."

"You wanted me to break up with you?" Chloe teased.

"Okay, what I'm saying isn't very clear, but bear with me. If I had been the intended recipient of this message, it would have meant that we'd been together before that."

Sanji looked so flustered that she burst out laughing.

"I've never heard anything so absurd. You're out of your mind."

"I think you need to be a little out of your mind in order not to lose your mind entirely."

"You can't imagine how much of what I've gone through the last few years proves you right."

"Did you call him back?"

"What are you talking about?"

"You know."

"How is that any of your business?"

"Deepak asked me to watch over you—I'm just doing my job as an elevator operator."

"Why did you tell me you were a businessman?"

"You live on the top floor of a fancy building. Isn't that reason enough?"

"You know, I think you're coming on to me, rather awkwardly, but . . ."

"But what?"

"You shouldn't worry about appearances so much. I know what I'm talking about."

"In my country, it's not just about appearances. People of different social standings don't spend time together. Would you have dinner with an elevator operator?"

Chloe gazed off into the distance.

"Let's change venues," she suggested. "Tomorrow, I leave the studio at five. You know where to find me."

Chloe left, and Sanji remained sitting on the edge of the fountain for a long time. Before he left the park, he saw that he'd missed a call from Sam and called him back. The investment bank Holtinger & Mokimoto had read their materials and agreed to meet with them. With shareholders like these, he could quickly raise the rest of the capital.

"Don't tell me it's too soon to celebrate! I reserved a table at Mimi's, one of the best restaurants in the city. The French food there will make your *pata vrap* seem disgusting by comparison."

"It's called *vada pav*, and what would you know about it? Anyway, I can't do tonight."

"If it's because of this Otis woman, invite her to come with us."

"That could be complicated—she weighs around six hundred and fifty pounds, and that's when she's empty."

Sam took a deep breath and hung up on him.

◆ ◆ ◆

When his shift began that night, Sanji didn't have a minute to himself.

He was sure he had seen the man who entered the lobby carrying a small suitcase somewhere before, but he couldn't say where. He left the desk to go greet him.

"Ninth floor, please," the professor said.

"Should I announce you?"

"No, it's a surprise. Is Chloe back?"

"I don't have permission to answer you. Those are my instructions," Sanji retorted, closing the elevator gate.

"And what is the source of these instructions?" the professor asked at the fourth floor.

Only then did Sanji recall having seen his passenger with Chloe at Claudette's.

"I'm not sure she likes surprises. In fact, a lot of women hate being surprised. I should have followed the rules," Sanji muttered, turning the handle the other way.

The elevator stopped abruptly between the seventh and eighth floors. In other circumstances, the professionalism shown by Mr. Rivera's replacement would have reassured, or even amused, Professor Bronstein, but he had just traveled five hours from the West Coast, and his sense of humor was as exhausted as he was.

"Please get the elevator moving again."

"Not until you tell me who you are!"

"Her father!" the professor answered curtly.

Sanji turned the handle back in a very dignified manner.

"My sincere apologies, I would have preferred for us to meet under better circumstances, but—"

"You have your instructions, yes, I'm aware," the professor interrupted. "Now, if you don't have any objections, I'd like to go home and greet my daughter, who, I assure you, will be very happy to see me."

"I'm very happy to see you too—that's not what I meant—good night, Mr. Chloe—that's not what I meant either," he stammered. "But I don't know her last name, I mean, your last name. Deepak always calls her Miss Chloe."

"Bronstein, Professor Bronstein!"

Sanji went back down, beet red. He had just gotten to the lobby when he was called to the eighth floor.

The Williamses were dressed to the nines in a tuxedo and an evening gown.

"Very chic," Sanji complimented them, leaving the couple flabbergasted.

Shortly afterward, the Clercs also left, worried about being late to the movies.

"What movie?" Sanji asked.

"*La La Land*," Mr. Clerc replied.

"I've heard it's very good. Apparently the actors really know how to dance," he concluded, escorting them through the lobby.

The Clercs exchanged amused looks under the awning and got into the taxi that Sanji had just hailed for them.

Mr. Morrison had given up his evening at the opera. In fact, he had given up going out at all. Since nightfall, he had been pacing back and forth in his living room, shooting stealthy, nervous looks at his couch every time he served himself a glass of whiskey.

In an even rarer occurrence, Mrs. Collins rang at 8:50. She appeared on the landing with a small suitcase in hand. She initiated the conversation, complaining that she hadn't been able to bolt her door.

"I can never do it! Usually Deepak does it for me."

Sanji offered to help, but Mrs. Collins replied that her locks were so unpredictable that she was afraid she wouldn't be able to open the door the next day.

"I'm not sleeping at home tonight," confided the charming elderly lady. "My friend on the Upper West Side is hosting a bridge tournament. Her parties always go late, and we drink a little more than we should, so I prefer to spend the night at her place."

"Don't get too tipsy if you want to win the tournament," Sanji advised.

"Thank you for your wise advice, young man," she said, closing the cab door.

By midnight, all the other owners had returned. When he took the Clercs up in the elevator, Sanji asked if they had liked the movie.

"Eet was a delightful musical," Mrs. Clerc replied with a smile.

Sanji enthusiastically recommended *Jab Harry Met Sejal* to them, a remake with much better dance numbers than the original.

And since Mrs. Collins wasn't staying in her apartment, Sanji used his set of keys and went to sleep in her living room.

The Day I Put Away My Prostheses

Every time I put them on, two blades penetrate my skin. Standing up requires superhuman effort, and taking a few steps makes me look like a misshapen robot.

When I stand, I don't feel like a woman anymore.

My prostheses will sleep in my closet, and I'll stay seated. I have to accept my life for what it is and stop pretending.

19

Mr. Mokimoto listened to Sam for two hours, taking notes from time to time. Suddenly, he tapped on the table with his pen, indicating that the meeting was over.

"Could you leave us for a moment?" the banker asked Sam.

To put Sam at ease, Sanji gave his friend an assuring smile to show that he could continue the conversation without him. Sam gathered his materials and went to wait in the hallway.

"Your associate was very convincing," Mr. Mokimoto said.

"But?" Sanji asked.

"Why do you think there's a 'but'?"

"There always is."

"I'd like to know the real reason you came up with this idea."

"I'm not sure you want to hear it—the business world isn't crazy about idealism. But since you asked . . . My algorithm doesn't work like the others. It doesn't deliver the information you expect, the kind that reinforces your own way of thinking. Well, it does that in the beginning, but only in the beginning. Then, gradually, it offers you different points of view, narratives, and impressions. It opens a window into other lives. My social platform pays more attention to human relationships than virtual ones. When you post something, whether it's photos of places you've been or things you like, users can really choose the privacy settings and be in control of their private life. Unlike Facebook, there's no algorithm deciding the order in which information appears to the user. And what's even more unique is that there are no ads. Our users aren't cash cows, and we don't steal their data. Basically, we do the opposite of all our competitors. It's not just what they have in common that brings our users together, but also their differences. Social networks function in a vacuum—they divide us, set us against each other, and support a caste system maintained by the dominant classes, a system that is eating away at India. Imagine what society could become if people listened to each other instead of insulting each other. We want to teach people to get to know each other, understand each other, respect each other, broaden their horizons, and to put out the fires of hatred that feed on ignorance."

"That's certainly an unorthodox approach."

"My family didn't hesitate to point that out to me, and I suspected your reaction would be no different. I've probably wasted all of Sam's hard work, but hypocrisy isn't my strong suit," Sanji added as he stood up.

"Stay—we're not finished. My oldest son is twenty-three. The day before yesterday, he told me everything he thinks is wrong about the way the government is running our country. America is more divided than ever, inequality is increasing, and those in power seem to lack the conscience to do anything about it. I'll spare you the rest because the criticism was directed at me. It's not unjustified, I admit. Programs for education, health, reducing poverty, protecting the environment, justice, civil liberties—my friends are destroying it all, methodically and relentlessly. Last week, the third-highest official in the nation congratulated himself for having passed tax reform that will let a teacher take home a dollar fifty more per week. Paul Ryan got half a million dollars from the Koch brothers after saving them a billion and a half in taxes. I'm not complaining—like all the magnates in this country, I benefit greatly from this reform, and I've rarely made as much profit as I have this year. So I asked my son to consider the following question:

179

How will he react the day when, as a responsible banker, I seize his house, his car, his health insurance, when I increase the cost of his children's studies, put a cap on his salary, or when I fire him and replace him with a machine that's more profitable than he is—basically, when I annihilate all his hopes for a decent life? Will he be angry, will he hate me? He answered that he already did. But his anger does nothing except cause more hatred and frustration in the world. I couldn't care less about his feelings, because, however noble they may be, there's no risk they'll prevent us from continuing to enslave his generation. We have acquired everything—industries, businesses, agriculture, banks, even information belongs to us. As for the political parties, we bought them a long time ago."

"Why humiliate your son like this?"

"So he'll realize that preaching vainly won't make him one of the good guys. So he'll stop thinking and instead stir up trouble as long as he's able; so he'll stop being rebellious and start revolutionizing his world; and above all, so he'll go out and start living!"

"What does all this have to do with me?"

"I'm getting to that. We have so much money that we don't know what to do with it anymore. But we've gone too far. My friends are buying democracies—their appetite for power is insatiable. Call it remorse, if you like, but I'd like to throw a monkey wrench into the works before it's too late. And I have the means. So tell your friend waiting outside to send me the contracts. You've got your money, if you'll accept an investor like me."

Sanji looked Mr. Mokimoto in the eye and then hastily left the room.

He sped past Sam, raced down the staircase of the bank, and took a taxi to 28th Street.

◆ ◆ ◆

Chloe was waiting for him on the sidewalk. Sanji apologized for being late, grabbed the handles of her wheelchair, and made a mad dash down the sidewalk, zigzagging between other pedestrians.

"Can you tell me what you're doing?"

"Racing with this bus," Sanji replied. "I bet you we'll beat it to the river."

"How do you know it's going toward the river?"

"I don't, but we are!"

"Would you like to tell me what has put you in such a good mood?" she asked when Sanji finally slowed down.

"Spending time with you isn't a good enough reason?"

"Shoot! I forgot my book in the recording booth, and I wanted to rehearse tonight."

"I'll go get it for you later."

"Why are you going to all this trouble for me?"

"I like to help people. Otherwise, I wouldn't be an elevator operator."

Before reaching the banks of the Hudson River, they passed under the old elevated train tracks of the High Line, which had been converted into a pedestrian path. Sanji looked up and admired the imposing metal structure. Chloe told him there was an elevator at 30th Street.

They strolled along the greenway, going south from Chelsea all the way to the Meatpacking District. They stopped and watched two joggers pass them by at a quick pace.

"I'm not saying this to brag, but a few years ago, I would have left them in the dust."

"Did you ever think about prosthetic legs?"

"I have two beautiful ones in my closet, with steel calves and ceramic feet. But they only improve the way people look at me, not the way I live."

"I wasn't talking about aesthetics, but standing up, walking again."

"Try spending a day up on stilts, and then we'll talk."

"You wouldn't need to wear them all the time. My father used to take off his glasses before he went to sleep. That said . . . sometimes he did forget them on his nose when he took a nap."

Chloe burst out laughing.

"What did I say?"

"You have a spontaneous way about you that's very disarming."

"And that's good?"

"Not for everyone, but for me, yes."

"There's nothing I want more than to disarm you."

"Please stop."

"Stop what?"

"This game of flirtation. It feels good now, but it will hurt later, like the prostheses."

"It's not a game. What are you afraid of—that someone might be interested in you?"

Chloe turned toward the seating area overlooking 10th Avenue a few yards away.

"See that couple watching us? They can't stop looking at my wheelchair."

"You're so vain!"

"Very funny, but I don't get it."

"You're always convinced that people's attention is focused on you. *I'm* the one they're watching—they're wondering if I'm your friend or your servant. Well, actually, I *am* your elevator operator."

"Very funny."

"You have nice wheels, but I have dark skin. What do you think shocks them more?"

Chloe looked at Sanji for a moment.

"Come here," she said, taking his hands and pulling him toward her.

She wrapped her arms around Sanji's neck and kissed him on the lips. A movie-style kiss, but a kiss nonetheless, and Sanji's cheeks turned from dark to crimson.

"There, now they know you're not my servant."

"Why do you care so much what others think of you?" Sanji asked.

"I don't give a flying fig what people think," she replied.

"Not even a flying one?"

"I just told you!"

"So why did you kiss me?"

And before Chloe could answer, Sanji kissed her back, a real kiss this time.

It took a moment for their heart rates to return to normal. They looked at each other in silence, both equally surprised. And then they began moving again without saying a word.

When they got back to the street, there were so many tourists that Chloe had a hard time making her way down the sidewalk. Sanji spotted an ice-cream shop. Since there were only stools at tall tables, he sat down cross-legged on the floor, facing Chloe's wheelchair.

"This is the first time a man has thrown himself at my feet," she said with a smile.

Sanji lifted up the bottom of her pashmina and made a dubious face, which amused Chloe more than it offended her.

"You've never asked what happened to me."

"Is that bad?"

"At first, I thought you were afraid to, and then . . ."

"Then what?"

"I thought you were being sensitive."

"Maybe I'm just self-centered and I don't care about what happened to you."

"That's also possible," she said.

Sanji looked at her and got up.

"I have something important to do before my shift starts. Can you get home on your own?"

"I should be able to manage."

"So before my carriage turns back into a pumpkin, allow me to bid you adieu, Miss Chloe."

He kissed Chloe on the cheek and left.

Sanji spent the night in the lobby, engrossed in the pages of the book he had picked up from the recording studio.

At the end of every chapter, he went outside the building, looked up at the ninth-floor windows, and then went back behind his desk to continue reading.

20

At eleven a.m. Monday, a policeman appeared in the lobby. Displaying his badge, he asked if a certain Mrs. Collins lived at this address.

"Did something happen to her?" Deepak asked worriedly.

The detective's only answer was to ask which floor she lived on.

The only time Deepak had ever dealt with the police, he had been thirteen years old, and the memory of being struck with a club had haunted his nights for a long time. In the elevator, the detective noticed how his hand trembled on the handle.

When Mrs. Collins opened her door, the policeman displayed his badge once again.

"You didn't waste any time—it's barely been an hour since I called you."

"Usually people say the opposite," Detective Pilguez muttered. "May I come in?"

Mrs. Collins let him pass by and glanced at Deepak, whom she had never seen so pale before. She led the detective to her living room and told him what had happened: when she went to get dressed that morning, she had discovered that a very valuable necklace had been stolen.

She was almost certain that it had still been in her possession just a few days before, because she had considered wearing it to a party at a friend's house.

"What's your friend's name?"

"Philomena Tolliver. We've known each other for ages. Every three months, she hosts a bridge competition. She's quite generous with the drinks, so I prefer to spend the night there."

The detective jotted down Philomena Tolliver's name and address in his notebook.

"Do you spend the night away from home very often?"

"Once every three months."

"Except for your friend and her guests, who else knew the date of this competition?"

"Her butler, the caterer (Philomena can't even make scrambled eggs), her super, maybe a few other people . . . How should I know?"

"In the taxi that you took to the party, did you mention that you weren't coming home that night?"

"I'm no spring chicken, but I haven't yet reached the point of talking to myself."

"During the day, do you go out at regular times?"

"Sometimes, in the midafternoon."

"Where do you go?"

"What does this have to do with your investigation? I go out for a walk—that's allowed, isn't it?"

"I'm not here to annoy you, ma'am, I'm just trying to draw up a list of people who could have known when your apartment was empty."

"Yes, of course. I'll try my best to help you," Mrs. Collins replied sheepishly.

"Where did you last see this valuable necklace?"

"Where I've kept it ever since my late husband gave it to me, in my jewelry box."

Mrs. Collins's walk-in closet was a disaster: clothes were scattered on the floor, towels were piled in one corner, and the dresser drawers were half-open.

"They sure did a number on you," said the detective.

Mrs. Collins lowered her head. Seeing her so unsettled, the detective felt sorry for her.

"A burglary is always more shocking than you expect."

"No, it's not that," Mrs. Collins murmured. "I'm a bit disorganized. My husband used to always complain about it. So I'm not really sure who's responsible for this chaos, the burglars or me."

"I see." The detective sighed. "Do me a favor: check that your necklace isn't buried in this mess. Don't touch the drawers—I'll take fingerprints, and I'll have to take yours, too, to rule them out in case we find anything."

"Of course," Mrs. Collins said apologetically. "Could you lend me a hand?"

"Certainly not! I'll inspect the locks. Is there a service entrance?"

"In the kitchen," Mrs. Collins said, pointing down the hallway.

He joined her a few moments later. The closet looked no better than before; the mess had just been piled differently.

"Is the necklace the only piece of jewelry that was stolen?"

"I don't know—the others are fake, so I don't keep track of them."

"So your burglar knew what he was looking for. But we still need to figure out how he got in."

"I hadn't managed to bolt the door. Picking the lock wouldn't be hard for someone who knows how to do it."

"There's no sign of forced entry. It's a masterful job, unless he had the keys."

"Impossible, they're always on me," Mrs. Collins declared, opening her purse.

"And you haven't noticed anything unusual or anyone following you recently?"

Mrs. Collins shook her head vigorously.

"Okay, I have all I need. You'll have to come sign a statement at the station. Are you insured?"

Mrs. Collins said she was. The detective gave her his card and asked her to call him back if she remembered seeing anything suspicious.

Detective Pilguez took advantage of Deepak's presence in the elevator to question him.

"You didn't notice anything abnormal over the last few days?"

"That depends on what you mean by abnormal," Deepak mused.

"I imagine there's never a dull moment in a fancy building like this. Have there been other burglaries?"

"Not a single one in the thirty-nine years I've been working here."

"Strange case," muttered Pilguez. "Do you have security cameras?"

"There are three. I guess you're going to ask me for the tapes."

"You guess correctly. Have any strangers come around recently? Guests, salesmen, or workers?"

"No one, except for two elevator technicians, but Mr. Groomlat and I were with them the whole time."

"Who's Mr. Groomlat?"

"An accountant who has an office on the second floor. He's also the co-op president."

"Do clients come to see him?"

"Very rarely. In fact, almost never."

"Any delivery people hanging around the hallways?"

"They can only get into the lobby—we're the ones who bring the packages up."

"'We'?"

"Mr. Rivera works at night, and I'm on during the day."

"When does your colleague arrive?"

"He hasn't been coming lately because he's in the hospital. He had a bad fall in the staircase."

"Well, well. When did that happen?"

"About two weeks ago."

189

"Who's his replacement?"

Deepak hesitated before answering.

"It's not a very complicated question," the detective insisted.

"My nephew, as of a few days ago."

"And where does your nephew live?"

"With me."

"He has no other residence?"

"Yes, in Mumbai. He's just visiting New York. When Mr. Rivera had his accident, my nephew kindly offered his services. The elevator can only be run by a qualified operator, which, in my colleague's absence, posed certain problems at night."

"Your nephew from Mumbai turns up, and he steps in at the last minute to replace your colleague who fell down the stairs. Things happen fast here. Does he have a work permit?"

"His papers are in order. The union gave us a training agreement, and Sanji is an honest young man. I can vouch for him."

"That's very nice of you, but it's still not an alibi. Okay, get me those tapes. With a little luck, they'll be more informative than you are. And ask your nephew to come see me at the station as soon as possible. I have a few questions for him."

Deepak went to get the tapes in the basement and gave them to the detective.

"This Mrs. Collins . . . does she still have all her marbles?" Pilguez asked.

"She's the most charming of our residents."

"Her husband's been dead for a while?"

"Mr. Collins passed away about ten years ago."

"When do the other owners get home? I need to question them, and I'd like not to make too many trips. This isn't exactly the crime of the century."

"You can find them all here in the early evening," Deepak replied.

◆ ◆ ◆

Chloe was going to make breakfast in the kitchen when she suddenly turned around in the hallway. No note had been slipped under the door overnight. Only when she left for the studio around ten did she discover her book on the doormat and a message scribbled on a bookmark.

I have a favor to ask you. Meet me at 6 at the corner, on the park side.

Sanji

◆ ◆ ◆

The recording session seemed to go on forever. The booth was hot, and the sound engineer wouldn't stop interrupting her: she didn't articulate well enough, she skipped a line, sometimes she read too fast and sometimes too slow. Around four, Chloe decided it was time to call it a day.

She stopped at home to change and thought Deepak was acting strange when she left the building. She wondered about it as she wheeled to the park where Sanji was waiting for her, leaning against the fence.

"We could have met in front of my building," she said.

"I didn't want Deepak to see me."

"To see you, or to see us?"

"I'd like to get a present for my aunt to thank her for hosting me. I have a vague idea of what she might like, but I wanted to get your opinion."

And since he wasn't on duty, Sanji offered to push Chloe's wheelchair.

"No, thanks, you're a crazy driver," she replied. "Where are we going this time?"

"Just two blocks."

"Are you related to Deepak?"

"What makes you think that?"

"Nothing in particular."

"Except we're both Indian—"

"It was a dumb question," Chloe qualified hastily.

"My aunt is his wife."

"So my question wasn't so dumb."

Sanji pushed open the door of a flower shop on the corner of University Place and 10th Street.

"You need my help to buy flowers?"

"I don't know which ones she'll like."

"My favorites are the old rose varieties, like these," Chloe said, in front of a bouquet of Abraham Darby roses. "But for your aunt, I have a better idea."

She led him to a pastry shop.

"A box of pastries! And Deepak can enjoy them, too."

"It's strange—you seem to know them better than I do."

"There's nothing strange about that. I pretty much grew up with Deepak around."

"And what about you? Which kind do you like?" Sanji asked in front of the case.

"I'd like some tea, if you'll choose it."

Over a pot of Assam tea, they shared two meringues and an awkward moment.

"I'm not used to this," Sanji finally said.

"Buying flowers?"

"Kissing a woman I barely know."

"I kissed you, and it's out of character for me, too, especially right after a breakup."

"In that case, we can just pretend it never happened."

"And how would we do that?"

"By acting like adults, for example."

"Says the man who sprinted me down the street the other day and can't select a bouquet of flowers by himself. But if that's what you want . . ."

Sanji leaned over the table to kiss Chloe, but she gracefully turned away.

"When Mr. Rivera is better, you'll go back to Mumbai, right?"

"If he gets better soon, yes."

"If not, you'll leave even sooner?"

"Two weeks at the most, maybe three."

"Then, yes, it might be better to just pretend."

"What's the distance between us, an ocean and two continents, or nine floors?"

"Don't be cruel, do you think a girl like me—"

"I've never met a woman like you."

"You said you hardly knew me."

"There are so many people who miss out on each other for stupid reasons. Where's the risk in stealing a little happiness? If the end of the world were scheduled for the day Mr. Rivera recovers, wouldn't it still be worth it to fully experience the time we have left?"

Chloe looked at Sanji, a fragile smile on her face.

"Try again," she said softly.

"To convince you to give us a chance?"

"No, to kiss me, and this time be careful not to knock over the teapot."

Sanji leaned toward Chloe and kissed her.

"It would be very unfair to Mr. Rivera if the world ended on the day he got out of the hospital," Chloe said as they left the pastry shop.

Detective Pilguez came back at six p.m. to question the residents of 12 5th Avenue.

Mrs. Zeldoff quivered with fear upon learning that a robbery had taken place in her very own building. She didn't provide the detective with any information. She couldn't put her finger on why, but she chose not to mention the suspicions that had recently been cast upon the elevator operators. Perhaps without them, the burglars would have gone after her apartment, too.

Mr. Morrison had a serious hangover. He hesitated before revealing that he thought he had seen a man of color in his underwear in the living room. The detective tallied up the empty bottles on the coffee table and replied that once, when he was on a bender, Donald Trump had shown up in a tutu and sung a song in his kitchen. It had been one of the most traumatic experiences of his life.

The Clercs had seen and heard nothing. Mrs. Clerc felt obligated to recount her activities of the last several days in painstaking detail, and the detective, who had little desire to hear the specifics, interrupted her. She was under no suspicion.

Mrs. Williams was even more talkative. She related what happened when the technicians came to modernize the elevator. In a few minutes, she declared that she had solved the whole thing. The elevator operators had sabotaged the equipment and then organized a break-in to terrorize everyone and make their presence indispensable, so that the co-op would give up on installing the buttons once and for all. The detective doubted that Deepak's colleague had thrown himself down the stairs at his age just to have a good laugh. Mrs. Williams smelled like medication, a repulsive odor that reminded Pilguez of the camphor ointment that his aunt Martha used to put on her varicose veins. That was enough to make her seem untrustworthy.

"I conducted my own investigation," she protested. "Coincidences are rampant in this building. I found out that our new elevator operator is related to Deepak. Don't you find that strange?"

"Must have been a tough investigation—he told me so himself before I even asked. My wife's goddaughter worked the phones at the police station last summer. Call it nepotism if you like, but it doesn't mean my wife committed a crime."

"Well, if you refuse to do your job, why are you wasting my time?" Mrs. Williams challenged him.

"You took the words right out of my mouth, lady," the detective replied before slamming the door on his way out.

Pilguez ran into Chloe Bronstein in the lobby and asked to speak with her in her apartment.

He told her what had happened and noticed that she was the only one to show any sympathy for Mrs. Collins. The detective inquired about the elevator operators, and Chloe asked him if Mrs. Williams had been spreading rumors again. For a year now, her xenophobia had been out of control. You only had to watch her husband's reporting on Fox to understand the depth of her convictions.

"You all sure get along great in this building," the detective said wryly. "You didn't see anything unusual from this window?"

"Why do you ask?"

"No reason—I just notice things. Something tells me we have that in common."

"Noticing isn't the same as judging, Detective."

"Have you encountered the new elevator operator?"

"What does that have to do with anything?"

"Why not a simple yes or no?"

"He's a considerate and generous man."

"That's quite profound for someone you've only known a short while."

Chloe looked at him, perplexed. This detective had a presence that she found reassuring. She had felt something similar when Sanji had lifted her from her wheelchair and put her into the cab. And this feeling had come back every time she had been with him.

Since she had nothing more to say, the detective left.

In the elevator, he asked Deepak if he had any idea how the burglar had gotten past him and into the building.

"It's a mystery. When we go upstairs, we always lock the lobby doors," Deepak explained.

After the detective had left, Deepak remembered the morning when he had brought clothes for his nephew and found him fresh and clean as a whistle.

◆ ◆ ◆

"What about my figure!" Lali scolded, a smile spreading across her face. "Why are you giving me these treats?"

"To thank you for hosting me."

"Considering what you're doing for us, I should run into the kitchen and bake you a three-layer cake."

"Can I ask you a personal question?" Sanji asked, sitting down at the kitchen table.

"Ask it and we'll see."

"How did you find the courage to flee India?"

"You're not asking it right. Fear makes people flee. Courage is what pushes you to move forward, to embrace a new life. Courage is hope."

"But you still had to give up everything."

"Not what was essential. Besides, I didn't flee, I left with Deepak. I hope you can see the difference."

"When did you know he was the one?"

Another smile lit up Lali's face—this time, a mischievous one.

"What's her name? Oh, please, don't play coy with me! Asking that kind of question means something is tugging on you right here," she said, pressing her index finger to Sanji's chest. "Does she live in Mumbai? No, of course not," she interrupted herself. "Otherwise you wouldn't be asking your old aunt."

Sanji remained silent.

"Well?" Lali continued. "What do you want me to say? When you know, you know. You can overthink everything, especially the reasons it's a bad idea, and put blinders on so you can't see what's right in front of you, but in reality, our only choice is to seize our chance or let it slip away. If I hadn't followed Deepak, I would have spent my whole life regretting it."

"You weren't ever afraid that you were too different?"

"I'm going to give you some good advice: if you ever find yourself in a place where everyone around you is just like you, get out of there as fast as you can. And by the way, considering what time it is, if you don't want Deepak to get cross, you should probably get going now."

Sanji looked at the kitchen clock and rushed into the bathroom.

He was only half an hour late to 12 5th Avenue.

Seeing the look on his uncle's face, Sanji decided to take the bull by the horns.

"We said eight o'clock!"

"That was the other day. Well, at least you look respectable today. Did you hear the news?"

"What news?"

"So you don't know?"

Deepak told him about the robbery.

"Incredible!" Sanji said with a low whistle.

"Unacceptable!" his uncle retorted. "Whatever trick you used to take a shower the other night, I hope you didn't forget to lock the door on your way out. I don't want to know any more about it. Be vigilant tonight. This burglar might have the crazy idea of coming back here."

Deepak handed Sanji the detective's card and gave him another piece of advice: the less you talk, the less risk there is of regretting what you said.

"He wants to see you tomorrow. Remember what I said. Meanwhile, go put your uniform on—I want to get home!"

Sanji turned the card over in his hands and put it in his pocket before going down to the basement.

21

Sanji had an hour to kill before his meeting with Sam. He stuck his hand into his jacket pocket and read the address on the card that Deepak had given him. The police station was on 10th Street between Hudson and Bleecker. Ten minutes to get there, fifteen minutes at the station, and twenty minutes to go meet Sam. Maybe he'd even be early for once.

He went up to the desk of the Sixth Precinct and asked to speak to Detective Pilguez.

"What do you want with Detective Pilguez?" inquired a man busy pounding the coffee machine with his fist.

"I don't want anything, but he wanted to see me."

The detective turned around and looked at him.

"Oh, yes, the case of the widow's necklace. The crowning glory of my career. Okay, follow me. I would offer you a coffee, but this piece-of-junk machine must be clogged."

Sanji wasn't sure he understood what was going on, especially what had put the detective in such a mood, but he followed him into an adjoining room and sat down on the chair that the policeman indicated.

"So, you're the replacement elevator operator at 12 5th Avenue."

Following Deepak's advice to the letter, Sanji simply nodded his head.

"The surveillance cameras had some interesting footage. You leave your desk at twelve twenty a.m., and you don't come back until six ten a.m. The next day is pretty much the same thing—you disappear between midnight and six a.m. Where were you?"

"I was sleeping."

"Okay, but where?"

"In the basement storeroom."

"Now that's strange, because you never appear in the basement hallway, which is also under surveillance. The next night, you stay at your desk, but then your movements become really intriguing. You leave the building just about every hour and come back a few minutes later. Since I'm curious by nature, I took the trouble of paying a visit to the restaurant across the street. I noticed they have a surveillance camera out front. And that's where it gets even stranger: you cross the avenue and hang out on the sidewalk looking at the windows. Were you counting the pigeons on the balconies?"

"Do you have any proof that this theft took place during the night?"

"Mrs. Collins told us she went out for two hours in the afternoon, but burglars are rarely active in the middle of the day. And your uncle assured us that he locked the door whenever he went upstairs, which is clearly not the case with you."

"That's not true—I do it as soon as the last resident comes home."

"Not according to the cameras, so you're not helping your case much."

"My case? Does this mean I'm a suspect?"

"Not a single crime in this building in forty years. I'm not making this up—your dear uncle told me. And then, bam! A few days after you're hired, there's a break-in, and a necklace disappears. Well, not necessarily a break-in—this burglar is a real Houdini, because the locks weren't forced. Maybe he just walked through walls. Unless he has a set of keys—like you. One of the owners thinks he saw a man hanging out in his living room in his underwear in the middle of the night. I admit that, given this guy's condition, a judge would require a blood test before accepting his testimony, and I doubt there's much blood in his alcohol. But you lied when you said you slept in the basement, and I still don't know where you were. So if all that isn't a reason to hold you, I don't know what is."

"You're going to hold me?" Sanji asked worriedly. "But you don't have any proof."

"Not yet, but I have serious grounds. So as long as a lawyer doesn't come and spring you, you're going to enjoy a complimentary stay in our hotel."

"I look the part, is that it?" Sanji challenged.

"Buddy, if there was a type who looked the part, that would sure make my job easy. But there *is* one thing that's bothering me. To commit a crime so clumsily, you'd have to be a real idiot, and you seem pretty bright."

Pilguez ordered Sanji to follow him. He had to fill out a form and get his picture taken.

"I thought it was always the motive that betrayed the guilty party," Sanji said.

"A necklace of this value is a pretty nice motive, isn't it?"

"What would I want with a necklace?"

"Fencing it would offer you half its value. If I had that much money, believe me, I'd know what to do with it. A quarter of a million dollars—how many years' salary is that for an elevator operator?"

"For an elevator operator, I have no idea, but for me, not a whole lot."

The detective stared at Sanji and handed him over to two uniformed officers. They took his fingerprints and then photographed him from the front and side.

Sanji asked to make a phone call, but the officers ignored him and locked the cell door.

The morning rush had ended, and Deepak had finally caught his breath when his phone started to vibrate. He sighed and went up to the ninth floor.

"You aren't coming down?" he asked when he saw that Chloe was facing him.

"Could you put this envelope out on the desk when you leave this evening?" she replied before thanking him and closing her door.

Deepak asked no questions. He spent the next hour gazing at his nephew's name written on the letter that Chloe had given him.

◆ ◆ ◆

At six p.m., a taxi stopped at the corner of Bleecker and 10th. Sam got out, along with a legal assistant from his firm.

"Let's go over it one more time," he said as they approached the police station.

"What you're asking me to do is totally illegal."

"Only if you're a bad actor."

"I'm not a lawyer, for crying out loud!"

"You handle legal matters, right?"

"That has nothing to do with it!"

"Look, we need to get my buddy out of here pronto. So you say you're his lawyer, you ask what the charges are, and you explain that they have no evidence against him and no grounds for holding him. If need be, you threaten to go and complain to a judge, and bingo! You bring him out to me."

"And if there *is* evidence against him?"

"Evidence of what? If Sanji found a hundred-dollar bill on the ground, he'd take it to the lost and found. It's just racial profiling—they picked the first guy who wasn't white, that's all."

The legal assistant wasn't listening to a word of what Sam said, as he was busy practicing his lines under his breath.

"You're really going to owe me one, I swear!"

"Refresh my memory: Who was it that arranged for you to meet the girl who works on the sixth floor? Marisa, Matilda, Malika . . ."

"Melanie, and all you did—"

"I got stuck planning a work dinner for eight people and finagled it so that you could sit next to her. And if I hadn't spent the evening praising your legal expertise, you would have had zero chance with her, so prove yourself; otherwise, I'll have every reason to tell her I got a bit carried away about your talents. I'm waiting, and every half hour, your reputation takes a dive!"

Thirty-seven minutes later, the legal assistant came out of the station, sweating profusely but with Sanji at his side.

"So?" Sam asked. "No, don't say anything—I know, the police department screwed up. It's disgraceful! Why didn't you call me sooner?"

"Because they didn't let me make a phone call all morning. The detective wanted to wear me down. He probably thought he'd get a confession."

"A confession to what? This is crazy! I can assure you, I'm not going to let this go. An entire day of meetings, canceled—can you imagine the damages?"

"If I were you, I wouldn't do anything," murmured the legal assistant.

"That's enough out of you," snapped Sam. "The lawyer act was for the police station—when I need your advice, I'll let you know."

"Very well, but you should know your friend is suspected of committing a crime in the apartment building where he works."

Sam looked at him, stupefied.

"What building, what work?"

"He's an elevator operator!" said the legal assistant.

Practically apoplectic, Sam turned toward his friend this time.

"We need to talk," Sanji mumbled.

◆ ◆ ◆

Sanji hadn't had anything to eat since the day before. After devouring a pizza in a nearby restaurant, he told Sam everything.

"Spending your nights in an elevator . . . you couldn't have found an easier way to chase after a woman who gets around in a wheelchair?"

"It wasn't premeditated—it was just a random chain of events."

"What kind of events?"

"You know full well I didn't take this necklace. Of course, I did have the opportunity—I slept on Mrs. Collins's couch the night she was away."

"You what?"

"In any case, it wasn't that night or the previous one that the burglar struck—I would have heard him."

"Oh, because you went into other apartments?"

"Just Mr. Morrison's, but he had no idea. He was absolutely sloshed, and I know, because I put him to bed."

"Any minute now, my alarm clock is going to ring, and when I tell you about the nightmare I had, you're going to bust a gut laughing."

"Tomorrow this will all be over, and you're right, we'll both have a good laugh over it."

"Well, before we start laughing, let me make a couple things clear to you. A burglary happens in a building where you . . . I can't even say it. You leave your fingerprints in the apartment where it happened, and you have no alibi. Tell me you have a set of keys, too, and I'll drive you across the Canadian border this very night. Do you know how the justice system works in this country? And wipe that idiotic smile off your face—this really isn't funny."

"But, Sam, I'm innocent."

"Innocent . . . and a foreigner. What's this necklace worth, anyway?"

"About the amount you want me to invest."

"That has to remain strictly between the two of us. I'm going to get you a lawyer, a real lawyer, and he'll easily show that, with what you're worth, you had no reason to steal anything."

"So the Indian elevator operator is guilty, but if they find out he's a wealthy man, then he's as white as snow? If I had to get out of it like that, I couldn't look at myself in the mirror for the rest of my life."

"Sanji, you're a real pain in the ass with your principles. I'm also at risk here—if my boss finds out what you're accused of, I'll be fired on the spot. So let's do things my way, and we'll deal with your remorse later."

"I'm going to bed. I'll figure it out tomorrow. Thanks for everything."

Since he had arrived in New York, Sanji had spent his nights on a backbreaking sofa bed, the marble floor of a lobby, the couches of an alcoholic and an absent widow, and now he'd spent the afternoon on a bench in a ten-by-ten-foot cell. Enough was enough, and he went to check in at the Plaza.

◆ ◆ ◆

Deepak was worried. At nine p.m., Sanji still wasn't there. He called Lali, who hadn't had any news of her nephew all day. Deepak wondered how to remedy the situation. After much reflection, he went into his storeroom and came back and hung a little sign that he had never used before on the knob of the elevator door.

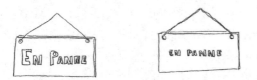

Then he went home.

22

A bath, room service, a movie on the giant TV screen in his suite, and a good night's sleep in a king-size bed with three pillows. All in all, the kind of night in a palace that should have taken his mind off things. That, in addition to the conversation he'd had with Mr. Woolward, the lawyer that Sam had hired, should have calmed him down. For a nonviolent jewelry theft, Woolward doubted the police would take fingerprints. And without any evidence or motive, he didn't think they would prosecute. You couldn't predict the course of a case like this, but he had assured Sanji there was no reason to be overly concerned.

Yet Sanji felt guilty. For having missed his shift, for not having had the basic courtesy to inform Deepak, for benefiting from the protection of a lawyer whom he never would have been able to afford as a real elevator operator. He would go apologize to his uncle that very morning. First, he made himself a cup of tea, took a quick shower, and got dressed. But as he was paying his bill, he suddenly wondered if he would still be welcome under Deepak's roof. On the way to 12 5th Avenue, Sanji was even more troubled. What had started out as a game was turning, day by day, into deception. He came up with another morning promise: he was done lying. He had to speak to Chloe.

◆ ◆ ◆

Deepak raised his glasses as his nephew entered the lobby.

"Did you let your aunt know?" he asked in a dismissive tone.

"Let her know what?"

"That you're alive. She didn't sleep a wink all night because she was busy calling every hospital in the city."

"I'm sorry, I'm out of the habit of letting my parents know when I'm not coming home at night."

"And you're insolent to boot! Why didn't you call? It was humiliating! I had to lie because of you."

"I couldn't call because I spent the night at the police station."

Deepak looked Sanji up and down.

"There are five-star jails now?"

"I changed at Sam's."

"I don't know who this Sam is," said Deepak with a sigh. "What did you say to that police officer to make him put you in jail?"

"I didn't say anything, but someone who advised me to weigh my words carefully told him that there had never been a burglary in this building until I started working here."

"I didn't say it like that."

"Well, that's how the detective took it."

Deepak frowned.

"This is a strange business. The thief didn't come in through the roof, so how did he get in and out without you or me seeing him?"

"I have no idea," Sanji replied. "Okay, I explained about yesterday—"

"That's your way of saying you're sorry?" Deepak grumbled, putting his hand into his pocket. "I'm being called. Wait here, it won't take long."

Deepak came back a few moments later with Chloe. He held the front door open and was surprised to see her stop in the lobby and remain planted in front of his nephew, and just as surprised to see Sanji gaze at her without saying anything.

"Nice suit," she said, then wheeled around and left through the open door.

She joined Deepak on the sidewalk and turned down his offer to hail her a cab. She wanted to get some air and would go to the studio by subway.

Deepak turned around and was almost knocked over by Sanji.

"What's gotten into you?"

"Which way did she go?"

"Remember my three rules?"

"Left or right?" Sanji insisted, grabbing his uncle by the shoulders.

"Well, she didn't go right," he replied, brushing himself off.

Sanji raced toward 9th Street, grabbing on to a street sign as he made a dangerous turn, and sprinted to 6th Avenue.

"Wait for me," he pleaded breathlessly.

Chloe was about to enter the crosswalk, but she turned around. Sanji caught up with her and stood in front of her wheelchair.

"I'm sorry I acted that way in the lobby, but Deepak was there—"

"I waited long enough last night," Chloe interrupted him. "You're going to make me late—move out of the way!"

"After you tell me what I did to upset you."

"Do I seem upset?"

"Frankly, yes."

"I didn't ask you for anything. I didn't expect anything. It was you who— So was it a game? A bet? To see if you could win over a girl in a wheelchair? You have every right to change your mind, but you could have had, if not the class, then at least the courtesy to answer me."

"I've been blamed for a lot of things since yesterday, but this is all news to me."

"The note I left on the desk for you. Maybe you didn't read it?"

"When did you leave this note?"

"Last night, so you would find it when you got there. I gave it to Deepak, and *he* at least is reliable. So don't try to come up with some elaborate excuse."

"I would've had a hard time reading it, because I was in jail."

"It just gets better and better! Every time I see you, it's one surprise after another. Did you run someone over?"

"Very funny! You probably know about the necklace. I'm their prime suspect."

"Tell me you're innocent!"

"I wouldn't go that far, but I'm certainly not guilty. What did your message say?"

"I'm not going to tell you. Now let me through—I'm really going to be late."

Sanji hailed a taxi. He expertly lifted Chloe out of her wheelchair, put it in the trunk, and sat down next to her.

"The corner of 28th Street and Park Avenue," he told the driver.

They arrived ten minutes later. Sanji accompanied Chloe to the door of the studio building.

"What did this letter say?" Sanji insisted.

"That I agreed."

"Agreed with what?"

"With your theory about the end of the world and a little interlude of happiness. You have twenty-four hours to find a way to redeem yourself. Come get me tomorrow at five thirty."

"Why not tonight?"

"Because I have plans."

◆ ◆ ◆

There's a strange paradox at the beginning of a love story. Full of fear, you hesitate to tell the other person they're constantly on your mind.

You want to give everything, but you hold back. You set happiness aside as if to preserve it. Budding love is both foolish and fragile.

◆ ◆ ◆

Although he was very late, Sanji arrived at his meeting relatively calm. Sam was used to him being on Mumbai time. But seeing him standing there with his elbows propped on the reception desk, Sanji expected the worst. This morning was certainly turning out to be full of accusations and excuses. But Sam did not reprimand him. In fact, he seemed to be in an excellent mood. He didn't say a word until they were in the elevator, when he asked Sanji to please press the button.

"Amazing!" Sam exclaimed.

"Very funny," Sanji replied.

◆ ◆ ◆

At the end of the day, Sanji went to take over from his uncle. They exchanged a few polite words, and Deepak left to go visit Mr. Rivera.

At the hospital, he hesitated to tell Mr. Rivera about the stolen necklace. But Deepak was a terrible liar, and when his colleague kept asking what was bothering him this time, Deepak told him everything.

"I didn't even know she had a piece of jewelry worth so much. I'm sure if it hadn't been a gift from her husband, she would have sold it a long time ago. She's not exactly rolling in money," Rivera explained.

"I didn't know. I don't get involved in their lives," Deepak answered absently.

"What are you thinking about?"

"How did someone get in without us seeing? We always stay at our post."

"Not always." Rivera sighed.

"And please don't ask if my nephew had something to do with it, because he didn't."

"I wasn't going to ask you that."

"I don't even want you to ask it to yourself."

"Then who was it, and how did they do it?"

"Which one of us is the detective-novel expert? You should be able to find the guilty party!"

"Let's proceed methodically," Rivera suggested in his best gumshoe manner. "The motive is obvious: money. Now, let's think about how the thief went about it . . ."

Sitting up in bed, Mr. Rivera became lost in thought while Deepak, on his chair, fell into a deep sleep. An hour later, he awoke with a start when he heard his colleague shout: "It was an inside job!"

"What are you talking about?"

"Think about it, for goodness' sake! If the cops had seen someone on the tapes, they would have already come back with a photo so you could identify the culprit. So no one went in or out, because the thief was already in the building! Since you can vouch for your nephew, it must be—"

"Must be who?"

"Nothing, forget it—I've had too many painkillers tonight."

"What are you talking about? You haven't taken a single one since I've been here."

"But I'm tired and you are, too."

Deepak got the message. He grabbed his jacket and left, more disturbed than he had been when he'd gotten there.

The state he found Lali in didn't do anything to calm his nerves. His wife was sitting at the kitchen table. The table wasn't set, and she hadn't made dinner.

"They put my nephew in jail," she stammered, on the verge of tears.

"They just held him overnight, my love," Deepak replied, kneeling beside her.

He held Lali in his arms and comforted her with all the tender affection he was capable of.

"They did it to intimidate him," he added. "They wanted to get a confession, but Sanji didn't give them one because he's innocent."

"Of course he's innocent. This country was a promised land for immigrants like us. We worked like dogs, out of duty and gratitude, and look what they do to us. Foreigners are treated like criminals. If this is the America of today, then I want to go back to India."

"Come on, Lali, calm down. It won't last."

"If an upstanding man like my nephew is arrested by the police, then what will become of us?"

"Just remember you didn't even know him a few weeks ago."

"My blood flows in his veins, so if I tell you he's honest, please just take my word for it!"

"Do I need to mention how your family treated us?"

Lali pushed back her chair and left the kitchen.

"This really isn't the time to try to get the last word!" she shouted, slamming the bedroom door.

Deepak shrugged his shoulders, opened the refrigerator door, and served himself the previous night's leftovers, a bowl of curried okra that he ate cold, alone in the kitchen.

That night, it was his turn not to get a wink of sleep. He brooded on dark thoughts. Maybe Lali was right. To wrap up their investigation, the police didn't need to catch the real criminal; they just had to point the finger at someone, and Sanji would fit the bill.

23

A storm rumbled over the city. The morning rush had been disrupted. Deepak's lobby looked like Noah's ark—almost all the owners were stuck there.

Deepak, whose umbrella had been blown inside out by the first assaults of the wind, was getting soaked. Undaunted, he waved his arm madly in the hope of hailing taxicabs. Rain was streaming down his neck, seeping under his uniform coat, and soaking his shirt so thoroughly that it stuck to his back. His uniform had lost all its splendor. When a delivery truck sprayed brackish water onto his pants, it was not just the weather that was stormy. Dull anger came over Deepak and grew minute by minute. And the police car that pulled up in front of him didn't make him feel any calmer.

"Missing monsoon season?" the detective asked sardonically as he lowered his window. "Here are the videotapes," he added, handing him a package. "Be careful, it's not waterproof. In any case, we didn't find anything interesting."

Deepak looked him in the eyes.

"I have information about your investigation."

The detective turned off the engine. He left his car double-parked and followed Deepak into the lobby where Mrs. Zeldoff, Mrs. Clerc, the Williamses, Mrs. Collins, and Professor Bronstein were waiting for the rain to let up. Some were scrutinizing the black clouds through the iron-and-glass door, while others were busy sending texts and e-mails in an overall atmosphere of nervousness and impatience.

Deepak stood in front of his desk and cleared his throat to get everyone's attention.

"I stole the necklace."

Suddenly, no one was thinking about the rain anymore.

"What are you talking about?" the professor said anxiously. "Not you, Deepak, this doesn't make any sense."

"No one asked for your opinion—let him speak!" Mrs. Williams cried out.

Deepak divulged all, explaining what had led him to commit such an act. His disappointment, the despair he felt when they had wanted to replace him with a crude machine, his humiliation when they accused him of sabotaging the equipment in question. He had been treated like a nobody, and despite his devotion, the owners for whom he had sacrificed everything had shown how little they thought of him, so why not just help himself? The theft of this necklace wouldn't bankrupt Mrs. Collins; her insurance would cover it. But what insurance did he have to take care of his aging wife? One year's salary?

"I should probably express remorse," he continued. "Maybe I'd get a shorter sentence. But I don't feel any. I even think I enjoyed paying you back in kind. And when I say 'in kind,' I mean as kindly as you repaid me for my services."

Deepak took off his cap and coat, placed them on the desk in a dignified manner, and held out his wrists to the detective.

Pilguez took out a pair of handcuffs from his pocket but didn't have the heart to secure Deepak.

"That's all right. You can put them on before we get to the station," he said, grabbing Deepak's arm.

The owners saw the elevator operator disappear into the back of the police car, and they were so shocked that they all came out under the awning to watch the vehicle make its way toward the arch.

When they went back into the lobby, Mrs. Williams was furious.

"Don't tell me it's starting all over again, except now we'll have to climb the stairs during the day!"

Professor Bronstein's cell phone rang.

"I'm going to get fired if I show up late to the studio—I don't care if it's raining, I'll take the subway if need be, but, please, Dad, tell Deepak to come and get me!" Chloe said.

The professor hung up. Seeing only one way to help his daughter, he addressed his neighbors.

"If there's still an ounce of compassion left in this building, I need volunteers to help Chloe."

Mrs. Collins was the first to speak up.

"What just happened right in front of your eyes wasn't enough for all of you?" she exclaimed. "Come on, get moving, let's go up!"

Mrs. Collins's demonstration of authority succeeded in mobilizing the troops. Even the Williamses joined the procession.

Soon Chloe heard a big commotion behind her kitchen door.

As everyone had their own idea of how to get Chloe downstairs, the descent took place in the most chaotic fashion possible. Her father carried her in his arms down to the fifth floor, where Mr. Zeldoff took over. Mrs. Clerc was in charge of carrying the wheelchair with the help of Mrs. Williams, who got her fingers caught in the wheel's spokes, whereupon Mrs. Collins informed her that she was useless. Mrs. Zeldoff stepped in, a big smile on her face. Awakened by this racket, Mr. Morrison appeared on the landing in his underwear and asked the question no one wanted to answer. What had happened to Deepak?

On the next floor down, Mrs. Williams took great pleasure in proclaiming that her suspicions had proven true; Deepak had confessed.

And Chloe didn't wait to reach the second floor to express her indignation.

"Impossible!" she shouted. "How could you let him do something like that—aren't you ashamed of yourselves?"

On the ground floor, Mr. Williams placed Chloe back in her wheelchair. A heavy silence filled the lobby.

"She's right," said Mrs. Collins. "We should be ashamed. Who among us could believe for one second that Deepak is a thief? Our suspicions wounded his pride, and so he confessed."

"Or he did it to protect his nephew," Mrs. Williams whispered.

But after a series of scathing looks from her fellow owners, she quickly lost interest in making this argument.

"That's settled, then," Chloe continued. "Since we all agree, it's up to us to get him out of this. Meeting tonight at six p.m. on the ninth floor. And someone should inform Mr. Groomlat. We're in this mess because of him. And, Mr. Morrison, please try to put some pants on before then."

No one dared challenge Chloe's claim to the first taxi that came by.

◆ ◆ ◆

At noon, Sanji got a text message that ruined his afternoon.

> Can't see you tonight. Let's say tomorrow.
> xoxo Chloe

Arriving at 12 5th Avenue early for once, he was astonished to find the lobby empty and worried when he didn't see his uncle. His worry only increased when he realized that the elevator was on the ground floor and the front door wasn't bolted. He rushed to the basement, checked the storeroom, called Deepak several times, and dashed up to the ninth floor.

Mr. Bronstein opened the door, and he could hear voices in the living room.

"Is my uncle with you?" Sanji asked, panting.

"Wait a moment, please, it would be better if she explains the situation," the professor replied.

Chloe appeared in the hallway a few moments later.

She told him what had happened that morning. Before Sanji had time to react, she assured him that no one doubted Deepak's innocence or why he felt he needed to make such a confession. They had come up with a plan to get him out of trouble.

"He's going to spend the night in jail? But he'll never recover from that!"

Chloe took Sanji's hand.

"I hope this doesn't come off as arrogant, but I believe I know him better than you do, or at least I've known him for longer. This was Deepak's way of expressing and venting his anger. Just before you got here, we told the police that he was innocent and that we had found the guilty party."

"Who the hell is it—I'll wring their neck!"

"It's a bit more complicated than that."

"I have to let my aunt know. When her husband doesn't come home, she'll be worried sick."

"I already took care of it. You should be with her. When I called her a little while ago to see how she was doing, she was on her way to the police station."

Behind Chloe, Mrs. Zeldoff poked her head into the hallway.

"I thought I heard your voice. You're here just in time—I was about to leave. Please take me to the third floor."

Sanji gave her a dirty look and left without answering.

Chloe followed him onto the landing.

"Will you be okay?"

"They don't deserve him!"

"They realize that now. When everything is back to normal, I'd love to have dinner with you."

Sanji gave her a half-hearted smile and left.

◆ ◆ ◆

Lali was waiting on a bench inside the police station. The desk officer had told her ten times that she wasn't allowed to stay there, and, ten times, she had calmly replied that, in that case, he could throw her in a cell so she could be with her husband. Eventually, he gave up on enforcing the rules. After all, if she wanted to spend the night there, it made no difference to him.

Sanji sat down next to her and put his arm around her shoulders.

"They'll let him out tomorrow morning, I promise."

"You're a policeman now?"

"I was worried when I didn't find him in the lobby, so I went up to see Chloe, and she told me what happened."

"You don't call her 'Miss Chloe' anymore?"

"The owners had a meeting in her apartment. They have a plan—I don't know what it is, but they seem confident."

"I'm sick and tired of hearing about those people!" Lali said sharply.

"Did you bring him clothes?" Sanji asked, seeing a small suitcase at his aunt's feet.

"For him and for me, too, along with all our savings to pay his bail. I even brought our passports."

"What do you need your passport for?"

"To leave! As soon as he gets out. I want to go back to India. I warned him that, after they were finished with you, they'd come after us."

"They didn't go after anyone. Deepak turned himself in. But his confession isn't believable. Let me take you home—this is no place for . . ."

"Go ahead and say it: for a woman of my age?"

"For my aunt."

Lali placed her hands on her nephew's cheeks and looked him straight in the eye.

"I've never slept without my husband . . . do you understand?"

So Sanji spent the night on the bench, watching over her.

At dawn, the desk officer went over to the coffee machine, punched it twice to turn it on, and brought them two coffees.

At seven a.m., Detective Pilguez entered the station, stopped in front of Sanji, nodded to Lali, and disappeared into his office.

At nine a.m., he returned to escort both of them into a little room and asked them to wait. For Sanji, the room brought back bad memories.

The door opened again shortly afterward, and Deepak took his wife in his arms.

"You should go home now, ma'am," instructed Pilguez.

"I won't budge until you release my husband."

"Your husband is free to go, but first the two of us have one little thing to take care of."

"Please," Deepak insisted. "Sanji, take your aunt home. I'll be there in a short while."

Sanji took the suitcase in one hand and Lali's arm with the other, and for once, she gave in.

◆ ◆ ◆

The police car parked in front of 12 5th Avenue.

"You're sure they'll all be there?"

"On a Saturday morning, definitely."

"Then go get them—I've got things to do."

But Deepak didn't want to follow orders anymore. He went down to the basement to comb his hair and found his uniform coat ironed and hanging in his locker.

He put on his uniform and went to ring every apartment's doorbell.

24

The lobby had once again been transformed into an impromptu meeting room. No one was missing. Even Mr. Morrison surprised everyone with his presence at what, for him, was an ungodly hour.

"Could you tell us why in the world we are being summoned by the police on a Saturday morning?" protested Mr. Clerc.

"Would you all rather have come to the station?" demanded Detective Pilguez.

Widespread murmuring made the answer clear.

"I've had investigations over the course of my career where, after several months, I still had no suspects, and here I have multiple guilty parties! If I believe the confessions that were made to me this morning, everyone here, or almost everyone, stole this necklace. This building is a regular jewelry store! Mrs. Zeldoff came forward first. I asked her how she managed it, and she revealed that she got into Mrs. Collins's apartment by distracting her with a far-fetched tale of vandalism. Then I got a call from Mr. Morrison, who explained that, because of a slight overindulgence in liquor, he went to the wrong floor and confused the necklace with one of his ties. Mrs. Clerc also called to tell me that she was ready to turn herself in, on the condition that she wouldn't have to reveal the motive that had pushed her to commit such a crime. What a lack of imagination! Mr. Bronstein had a financial motive; apparently they're pinching their pennies up on the ninth floor. But the prize goes to Mrs. Williams, who was evidently wild with jealousy since her husband had never given her such a valuable jewel. Since I'm sure that none of you can show me this damn necklace that you all allegedly stole, I'd like to know what made you think I was a complete idiot?"

The owners all frantically exchanged glances.

"Deepak is innocent," Mr. Bronstein proclaimed. "But since he turned himself in, we have no other choice but to block the investigation. Whether you believe us or not changes nothing—with so many confessions, you can no longer hold him responsible."

"I could charge all of you with obstructing a police investigation, making false statements, conspiracy, and—why the hell not?— possession of stolen goods."

"I convinced everyone to do it. I'm the only one responsible," replied the professor.

"That's not true!" Chloe objected. "It was my idea, and I'm ready to suffer the consequences."

"I told you it was irresponsible and stupid!" hissed Mr. Williams. "I admit I had a moment of weakness. My wife complains about everything already, so imagine what my nights will be like if we can't use the elevator again."

"I'm still convinced his nephew did it," Mrs. Williams interjected to save face.

"You're a petty person, Mrs. Williams—bitter, frustrated, manipulative, and mean," Mrs. Zeldoff blurted out, to everyone's surprise.

"I forbid you to speak to my wife that way!"

"I don't need your permission to say out loud what everyone already thinks," she continued, for nothing could stop her now. "You're a fine pair, a racist wife and a husband who reports for a vicious propaganda network, selling hatred. Poisonous snakes, the two of you!"

And the meeting had more surprises in store.

"Deepak's nephew isn't your thief!" Mr. Groomlat cut in, restoring order.

"What do you know about it?" asked the detective.

"Do you really think I would have let the co-op hire someone without first doing my homework? Who do you take me for? I conducted an investigation, too, especially since everyone was accusing me of negligence on account of this damn mechanism."

"What mechanism?"

"Don't worry about it, we ordered another one. What matters is what I found out. The young man that Mrs. Williams is wrongfully accusing had no reason to go and swipe Mrs. Collins's little trinket!"

"Oh, yes, it's only worth half a million dollars—a trinket indeed!" scoffed Mrs. Williams.

"Granted, but Deepak's nephew is worth around fifty million. He's richer than all of us put together, and I should know—I do your taxes. Why such a wealthy man chose to live such a bizarre double life, I have no idea, but since it was convenient for all of you . . ."

The Williamses, the Clercs, Mrs. Collins, Mr. Morrison, the Zeldoffs, and Detective Pilguez were all speechless. Chloe most of all. Their faces turned toward the desk, and they all realized that Deepak had slipped out.

The detective left, promising that he wasn't finished with them. Mr. Williams asked if they needed to help Chloe up to the ninth floor. The professor turned around sheepishly, only to discover that his daughter had also disappeared.

"What a relief!" exclaimed Mr. Morrison. "I'm going to go enjoy the rest of my day. Don't wake me up unless it starts raining whiskey!"

Sanji's cell phone vibrated, and a text appeared on his screen.

Where are you?

Sleeping.

Not anymore.
I need to talk to you.

You can call me.

But I need to see you! Meet me
at our pastry shop.

We agreed on dinner!

I can meet you in Spanish Harlem.

I haven't been staying there
since Deepak got back.

So where are you?

At the Plaza.

What are you doing at the Plaza?

Making up for a pretty significant sleep deficit.

Room number?

722.

◆ ◆ ◆

Mrs. Collins knocked on the door to Mr. Rivera's room. She came in and sat down on the bed. Mr. Rivera put his book down on the night-stand and stroked her cheek.

"Why do you look so upset? Did the doctors tell you I only have a few hours left to live?"

"The doctors didn't tell me anything because I'm not your wife."

Rivera gazed at Mrs. Collins sadly.

"It was you, wasn't it?"

"Yes, this time it wasn't the nurse," she replied.

"But why?"

"Because all this is my fault. Your accident, your wife being alone while we were together, her care that you can't pay for anymore. I feel so guilty."

"For showing me the affection I so desperately needed, or for making my life worth living again? I'm seventy-one years old—do you think, at my age, I don't know what I'm doing? My wife has forgotten I exist. Every time I visit her, she thinks I'm the painter or the plumber, or sometimes her doctor if she's in a good mood. Without you, I wouldn't have been able to stand it. It's about time I tell you a big secret. I've loved you since the day I first entered that building. If you only knew how many nights I came back down to the lobby furious that I wasn't the husband I had just taken up to the sixth floor. And when he died, I waited for a long time before I dared—"

"It was March 21," she interrupted him. "You told me, 'Mrs. Collins, you look beautiful.' I had just turned sixty-five, so you better believe I remember that! If you only knew how many nights I wished you were the one coming home from the office and saying, 'Hi, honey.' Sometimes love isn't right on schedule. But the important thing is that it gets there eventually, right? I'm such a coward—when I found out they had arrested that young man, I froze, I didn't say anything. But after Deepak's confession, which was brave but ridiculous, I was determined to tell the police everything. And then my neighbors confessed, so I thought this madness that came over me would finally solve our problems. But the detective isn't finished, and I've done enough harm as it is. I came to tell you goodbye. It's high time that I turn myself in."

"You know what Deepak told me recently? That it would be a good idea for a detective novel to end without the guilty party getting caught. At the time, I said it was stupid, but maybe he's right—it's not such a bad idea after all."

◆ ◆ ◆

Sanji was waiting for Chloe in front of the Plaza.

"You gave up on Spanish Harlem?"

"Not exactly. When they let Deepak go, I took Lali home. When he called to tell her he was on his way, I wanted to give them some time together."

Chloe looked up at the opulent façade of the Plaza.

"Why did you pretend to be an elevator operator?"

"To be near you at night, without bothering you. You're convinced that people only see your wheelchair—but I'm also afraid of how people see me."

"Afraid of what?"

"I didn't lie about anything. You're the one who didn't believe me."

"Were you afraid I'd judge you?"

"I was afraid a woman like you couldn't love a man like me."

"What does that mean, a man like you?"

"A foreigner who lives on the other side of the world, a man who's always late for everything, especially when it comes to love, and who's never felt this before meeting you."

"Felt what?"

"How are you going to get back to your apartment? Do you want me to go with you? I can pretend to be an elevator operator at least one more time."

"I have no desire whatsoever to go back home."

The Day I Slept
in a Palace

Sanji took me into his arms and kissed me. He lay down next to me and undressed me on the bed. It was the first time I felt his desire. I felt his lips on my skin, my breasts, my stomach. He's wonderfully strong, and gentle, and skilled. He kissed my thighs, and we made love.

We stayed in the room until the next morning. I called my father and said that while Deepak was gone, I had decided to stay with a friend. He didn't ask for any more details, which was good, since I could never lie to him.

◆ ◆ ◆

We had breakfast in bed. The bathtub in the suite was so big that we were able to take a bath together.

I didn't have a change of clothes, and Sanji wanted to take care of that. It's funny that a man who pays so little attention to his appearance has such good taste. We walked along Madison Avenue, and he picked out a dress, a long skirt, a top, and even a set of lingerie. I let him do it.

I always used to make fun of scenes in movies where a young couple experiences the first thrills of love. Big mistake, to paraphrase Julia Roberts. Big. Huge! We went boating on the lake. Sanji was absolutely determined to feed the swans—it was impossible to hold him back. As soon as he saw one, he steered us right up to it. He pulled his arms toward his chest as he rowed, tensing his legs, his arm muscles flexing. I confess it was irresistibly exciting, and the boat sped across the water as if we were racing. On the grass, we ate what remained of our lunch—sandwiches without bread, since it had all gone to feeding the swans. We snuggled under my pashmina, but the heat became unbearable, so we basked in the rays of the spring sun instead.

We had tea at the Blue Box Cafe at Tiffany's. I would have loved to wear a little black dress in that blue room, to hum everyday words in a convertible, to pretend for a moment that I was Audrey Hepburn, even if I wouldn't have traded Sanji for George Peppard, not for anything in the world.

Sanji insisted on seeing New York from the top of the Empire State Building. It was just what we needed to make our day together as perfect as a postcard, and we got to cut the entire line. It's only fair that my life has its advantages from time to time.

We went to South Street Seaport to take a water taxi at sunset. On the river, you can see all of downtown Manhattan's marvelous architecture. Sanji got a cramp in his neck from looking up as we passed under the Brooklyn Bridge, and when we came close to the Statue of Liberty, he was giddy with excitement. He promised to show me the wonders of Mumbai one day. I looked down and didn't say anything. I didn't want to think about tomorrow.

We had dinner at Mimi's, a French restaurant in Soho. The food was wonderful. I insisted on paying. Sanji objected that it was against his principles, but in the end, he agreed for fear of seeming old fashioned.

We came back to the Plaza at midnight. Sanji told me he would go back to work in the building the next day. I couldn't remain a prisoner in my city forever because of an elevator. And because my father was leaving to give a lecture in Texas, I suggested to Sanji that he join me once all the owners were back in their apartments.

We cuddled up to each other, and before sleep carried me away, I realized that I had missed such tenderness perhaps even more than my legs.

25

On Monday morning, everything seemed to go back to normal. Deepak entered 12 5th Avenue through the service door at 6:15 a.m. He smoothed his hair, dusted off his uniform, and adjusted his cap before glancing at himself in the little mirror on the door. Then he went up to the ground floor to clean the inside of the elevator. First the woodwork with a soft cloth and polish, and then, with a different cloth, the copper handle.

Rush hour was quieter than it had ever been in thirty-nine years. On each trip, all that could be heard was the hum of the motor, the whistling of the counterweight, and the slight squeaking of the gate, even though he'd just oiled it.

That Monday would be full of big decisions, and Deepak was the first to declare his.

Shortly before ten, he rang the bell at Mr. Groomlat's door and tendered his resignation.

"I'll stay on duty until the equipment is received and installed," he said without betraying the slightest emotion.

The accountant looked over the letter Deepak had given him.

"What about your goal?" he asked.

"You know about that?"

"Everyone knows about it."

"My wife is what gives my life meaning. All the rest is just pride," Deepak replied as he left. "I only ask one thing: if they happen to suggest a goodbye party, please dissuade them. I don't want one."

When Chloe appeared in the lobby a little after ten, wearing a pretty dress that he had never seen before, Deepak complimented her and told her that he would leave his job in six weeks' time at the most. This time, he was the one to take her hand.

"We'll always have wonderful memories, Miss Chloe. You've meant a lot to me. I'll never forget what you did."

Seeing her eyes brimming with tears, Deepak left it at that.

◆ ◆ ◆

Sanji shared his big decision with Sam, who listened without interrupting.

"Are you finished?" he finally asked.

"I think I've explained it all to you."

"One little question has been nagging at me ever since the day you made me eat that disgusting hamburger. Are you on drugs?"

"That's not funny."

"What's funny—hilarious, even—is that you want me to go manage your company in India while you become the head of the American branch."

"The idea makes a lot of sense. Here, everything still needs to be developed. Over there—"

"In other words, I would be your boss?"

"In other words, yes!"

"It's tempting. And since I speak Hindi fluently, managing a company with over a hundred employees will be the easiest thing in the world. I can already see myself in the sales meetings!"

"Everyone is bilingual in Mumbai."

"Sure, but understanding your English is another story. And let me guess: this girl you met has nothing whatsoever to do with your decision."

"She has a lot to do with it. Lali, too."

"How is your aunt involved in all this?"

"It's a long story. So, do you agree?"

"My first instruction as your boss is to ask you to leave me alone— go take a walk, or, no, actually . . . ," Sam said, scribbling something on a piece of paper. "Go visit these offices. They're for rent, and the price seems reasonable. I need to think. Before you leave, just sign these contracts with Mr. Mokimoto. Gerald will give them to you."

"Gerald?"

"My future assistant. His office is at the end of the hallway, you can't miss it."

Sam stationed himself at the window and waited for Sanji to get into a cab. Sam had sent him to IKEA in New Jersey, and until his friend figured out that he had been had, Sam would have the morning to himself.

◆ ◆ ◆

At eleven a.m., Sam entered the lobby of 12 5th Avenue and asked to be taken to the ninth floor.

"Is she expecting you?" Deepak asked warily.

"I'm a friend of Sanji's," Sam answered.

◆ ◆ ◆

On his way back from New Jersey, Sanji left Sam a very angry voice mail. If he wasn't even capable of giving him the right address in a New York suburb, he would have serious problems in Mumbai! Despite heavy traffic, he arrived just in time for the meeting he had set up with Mr. Woolward, his lawyer.

◆ ◆ ◆

At seven p.m., Sanji went to take over for his uncle, who told him that he had resigned that morning.

"You're under no obligation to keep working here," Deepak said, "and it's up to you to choose when to stop. To do things properly, I'd prefer to give the owners forty-eight hours' notice. I can never thank you enough for what you've done for us. Especially for me. I don't know if I can ever repay you."

"I know how," Sanji replied. "Maybe you could teach me your perfect cricket throw."

Deepak looked at him with evident pride.

"You're serious?"

"I realize it's a lot to ask, but you know what they say, never let the fear of striking out keep you from learning cricket from your uncle—"

"Sunday at two thirty on the field, and come dressed like a true cricketer—otherwise, no lesson, understood?"

"Does Lali know that you quit?"

"She knew I would make this decision before I did."

"And climbing Nanda Devi?"

"In the end, I think that having dreamed about it for so many years makes letting go of it more meaningful."

Deepak patted Sanji on the shoulder and, overcome by a sudden wave of emotion, hugged him.

He left his nephew and dashed off to the hospital.

"You did what you had to do," insisted Mr. Rivera.

"You're saying that because I didn't give you any choice. I should have talked to you first, but it wouldn't have changed anything."

"Given how stubborn you are, I'm sure you're right, and besides, I'm relieved. Last night, I decided to retire, too. Now that my wife's care is covered, I can afford to stop working."

"If you have the means, you might as well," Deepak said absently, picking up the newspaper that was lying on the floor near the bed.

His nonchalance exasperated Mr. Rivera so much that he sat up and snatched the paper out of Deepak's hands.

"Aren't you going to ask me how I can afford it?"

Deepak glanced at his watch and gave him a smug smile.

"I thought you would hold out for at least five minutes. I'm going to blame this on your medication."

"I have a secret to tell you, but this is just between you and me—will you promise?"

"Isn't that the idea of a secret?"

"I told you it was an inside job—"

"That's your big secret?" Deepak interrupted with a sigh.

"Let me finish! The necklace was never stolen. She wanted the insurance money. She took that risk for me, and I want to devote myself entirely to her."

"Thanks for sharing, but I figured that out a long time ago."

"Sure you did!" Mr. Rivera scoffed. "Always so proud."

"There's an old Indian proverb: 'Whoever steals an egg won't wait long to eat the chicken.' Want to hear a real secret? Your lady friend is also the one who sabotaged the equipment, Miss Chloe was her accomplice, and I erased the evidence."

Leaving his colleague with an astounded look on his face, Deepak retrieved the newspaper from the floor and stood up.

"A little subway reading. I'll leave you to your detective novels—I'm going home to my wife."

◆　◆　◆

Sanji waited until midnight to lock the front door of the building. He had taken Mr. Morrison upstairs a few minutes before. Though the inebriated gentleman had tried to start a conversation, Sanji took no risks, and shouted in his ear to prevent any inconvenient and cumbersome drowsiness in the elevator.

He went up to the ninth floor and rang Chloe's bell three times, but the door remained closed. Disappointed, he figured he had taken too long to close up and she had fallen asleep. Feeling a bit sad that she hadn't texted him, he went downstairs to spend the night in the lobby.

◆ ◆ ◆

When Deepak arrived the next morning, Sanji rushed off to his first meeting. As he left the building, he looked up toward the ninth-floor windows, hoping to see the silhouette of a woman he was already missing far too much.

Mr. Woolward was waiting for him at a deli near his office to share what he thought to be excellent news.

"Your uncles wasted no time in replying to the e-mail I sent. They're so afraid of having you on the board of directors of the Mumbai Palace Hotel that they're offering you a deal: five percent of your shares, and they're prepared to finance your projects in the US."

"Tell them I refuse," replied Sanji.

"Don't you want to at least consider it?"

"It's no use. They wanted war, and I'll give them two fronts to fight on. What they're afraid of now is the lawsuit I filed in India for my aunt to get her rightful share of the inheritance. When that happens in a few months, we'll have equal ownership with those old crooks."

Sanji thanked Woolward and hurried off to Spanish Harlem for his second appointment of the day.

His third meeting was with a real estate agent in Soho.

Sanji wanted to rent a loft with a view of the Hudson.

His final appointment took him back to 12 5th Avenue.

◆ ◆ ◆

"What's this? You're early!" exclaimed Deepak upon seeing his nephew.

"You're never satisfied. I didn't come to start my shift. I'm going up to the ninth floor."

"She's not there," Deepak replied.

"No problem, I'll wait."

Deepak cleared his throat and opened his desk drawer.

"Miss Chloe asked me to give you this," he said, handing him a letter.

"Better late than never! It's a bit old, and I already know what's in it."

"I doubt it." Deepak sighed. "She gave it to me this morning."

Sanji grabbed the envelope and slipped outside to stand under the awning.

> *Sanji,*
> *Of the two of us, I'm the selfish one; I never asked you about your past or what brought you to New York. I didn't know anything about your childhood or the path you've traveled. Sam came to see me this morning. Don't blame him for doing what real friends do. This crazy idea you had would have been entirely to his advantage, and it took an honest heart to tell me about it.*
>
> *We've never talked about what happened to me, and I've liked it that way. I didn't want to talk about it to anyone, not even the therapist who mentored me. The essential thing was to put my life back together again. But ever since I ran into you in the park, I've been living in this interlude of happiness, and I think that*

means I should confide in you. Yes, I liked you as soon as you sat down on that bench. Otherwise, do you really think I would have spoken to you out of nowhere like that? I was right—there's always some melody playing when two people meet. So here is the story of the day my watch stopped.

There were thousands of us on the starting line. And just imagine—a few weeks earlier, I was supposed to be on my way to Florence. But life had other plans. The morning started off beautifully: the sky was a dazzling blue, and a light breeze was on my side. Some people were running for organizations, others to make their families proud, or, like me, to prove they could beat their own records, not just beat other runners. That's the spirit of a marathon.

2:47: Commonwealth Avenue. A right turn onto Hereford Street, and then a left.

2:48: I finally got to Boylston Street, the home stretch. Flags from all countries fluttered in the breeze. Behind the barriers, people cheered us on: "Yeeeeah!" "Only a hundred yards!" "Only fifty yards!" "You can do it!" "You're almost there!" "We're rooting for you!"

2:49: I was running clumsily along, completely exhausted, like a broken puppet being pulled by sheer willpower. But I was determined not to give up so close to the finish line. I went over to the barriers to catch my breath, without worrying about the people behind me, and suddenly . . .

2:50: A bomb exploded, lifting me off the ground.

Acrid smoke floated above the sidewalk where the blast had thrown me. For a few seconds, I didn't believe the blood I was soaked in was my own, and then a man rushed over to me and took off his belt. I didn't under-stand what he wanted with me. His mouth was forming words, but I couldn't make them out. I only heard a piercing whistle. I sat up and saw him put a tourniquet above my knees. He was yelling to someone to press as hard as possible on my shredded flesh. The blood spurted out to the rhythm of my heartbeat. I turned my head away and saw dismembered bodies and burning cloth-ing, I heard shouting and moaning, I thought that I would die and never get to go to Florence. And then I could only watch the others, not because I was brave but because watching the horror around me made me believe that none of this was real, and that was what kept me alive. They put me onto a stretcher as people were running in every direction, and a woman said that my lips were turning blue, I had lost too much blood. A dark veil drifted over me, I felt a sucking inside my body, and then nothing.

It's strange, but the most memorable part of it all was seeing my parents together when I woke up in the hospital, and my father's tears.

Sanji, just as I didn't want to give up on that race, I can't let you give up on what you have built.

It only takes a short while to realize the value of a man like you. You challenged me once to tell you if the distance between us was an ocean or nine floors. It's much bigger than that: exactly sixteen inches.

It is time for me to visit Florence. When you read this letter, I will be on my way to Italy. There are so many things I promised myself I'd do. It's thanks to you—or it's your fault—because in your room in the Plaza where we made love, you gave me back my freedom and you granted me wings.

There are so many people who miss out on each other for stupid reasons. You're the one who taught me this. But that didn't happen to us, and the moments of happiness you were talking about have been ours. I will hold them in my heart, right where I will always keep a part of you.

Forgive me for writing instead of telling you this in person. I'm no good at goodbyes.

One day, I'll go for a stroll in the streets of Mumbai, we'll breathe the same air, and I already know that will make me happy. Who knows—maybe we'll run into each other in a park.

With love,
Chloe

◆ ◆ ◆

"She left this morning with a suitcase. She made me swear not to call you," explained Deepak as he joined Sanji under the awning.

Sanji folded the letter and put it in his pocket.

"I've been an idiot."

"Three rules. I asked you to follow three little rules. Was it really so hard?"

"Yes," Sanji replied.

"Wait for me here—I'll be back in a moment."

Deepak reappeared in his street clothes.

"Come on, Lali expects us for dinner. Since Miss Chloe doesn't need my services anymore, the others can just take the stairs."

Sanji hailed a cab, but as Deepak was a man of habit, they took the subway to Spanish Harlem.

Lali had set three places and prepared her husband's favorite dish.

The beginning of the meal was silent, but facing his aunt's probing look, Sanji ended up telling her everything.

"*You* should have talked to her, not Sam!" Lali protested. "You should have told her that you wanted to be with her more than anything."

"What difference would it have made?"

"All the difference in the world, you idiot. Did you listen to anything I told you?"

"May I inquire what you told him?" Deepak asked innocently.

Lali ignored him and continued speaking directly to Sanji.

"And why should it always be a one-way street—why should we always be the ones who have to leave everything to go live in another country?" she protested.

"Lali, mind your own business," Deepak interrupted.

"My nephew's fate isn't my business? When we were his age, wouldn't we have wanted a family member to help us?"

"How big is Florence?" Sanji asked.

Lali turned toward her husband and stared at him intently.

"Under no circumstances," said Deepak.

"I give you one minute!" she ordered, taking his plate.

Deepak wiped his mouth, angrily placed his napkin on the table, and for the first time in his thirty-nine-year career, broke the most sacred of his three rules.

"Miss Chloe is at her mother's in Connecticut. Just so you know, soon after telling your aunt to live her life without me, I changed my mind and told her we should go start a new life together. But what's the advice of an old elevator operator worth? And since everything has gone to hell around here, I'm going to bed!"

26

Day was breaking over the Merritt Parkway.

When the car reached Greenwich, the pale-pink light of dawn and the glare of headlights were all that illuminated the road.

At the end of a long street, a house built of light-colored wood appeared behind silvery pines.

Mrs. Bronstein opened the door and studied Sanji standing at the threshold. He apologized for arriving so early. She took a pack of cigarettes from the pocket of her robe and asked if he had a light before locating her own lighter.

She inhaled and looked him up and down once more.

"It's not that early—we spent all night talking in the living room. You can go in. I'm staying out here. My daughter doesn't let me smoke inside."

The embers were glowing in the hearth. Sanji asked Chloe if she wanted him to put on another log. She preferred that he come and sit next to her.

No one overheard their conversation, although Mrs. Bronstein showed up a short while later and suggested that her daughter go visit Mumbai for a few weeks instead of moping around on her couch.

Two or three weeks of happiness—what did she have to lose?

And as Mrs. Bronstein was a cultured woman, she quoted an Indian proverb before going off to bed: "In love, beggar and king are equal."

Epilogue

Lali and Deepak left Spanish Harlem. Lali is on the board of directors of the Mumbai Palace Hotel. Deepak took charge of a team of elevator operators in the hotel and oversees the flawless maintenance of three manual elevators. He accomplished his goal six months after his arrival and is now dreaming of Kangchenjunga, which measures 8,586 meters.

Mr. Rivera moved to a more modest altitude on the sixth floor of 12 5th Avenue. Wishing to make their relationship official, Mrs. Collins told Mrs. Zeldoff about it in confidence.

When Mr. Rivera's neighbors meet him in the elevator, they all wait respectfully for him to press the button.

As for Chloe and Sanji . . .

Mumbai, May 24, 2020

Your father held my hand as I gave birth to you.

I awoke in a hospital bed where, for the second time, my life was transformed.

Each of our paths in life has its ups and downs, as your great-uncle Deepak reminds us every morning.

I've learned something that I never would have guessed. When we reach the point we think is the lowest, life has an unsuspected wonder in store for us: life itself. And you are the proof.

This diary is for you.

Love,
Your mother

P.S. Monday, April 15, at 2:50 p.m. . . . . I will never understand why. But Boston Strong.

Acknowledgments

Pauline, Louis, Georges, and Cléa.

Raymond, Danièle, and Lorraine.

Susanna Lea.

Emmanuelle Hardouin.

Kate Deimling.

Elizabeth DeNoma and the Amazon Crossing team.

Cécile Boyer-Runge, Antoine Caro.

Caroline Babulle, Elisabeth Villeneuve, Lætitia Beauvillain, Sylvie Bardeau, Lydie Leroy, Joël Renaudat, Céline Chiflet, and the entire team at Éditions Robert Laffont.

Pauline Normand, Marie-Eve Provost, Jean Bouchard.

Léonard Anthony, Sébastien Canot, Danielle Melconian.

Acknowledgments

Mark Kessler, Xavière Jarty, Julien Saltet de Sablet d'Estières, Carole Delmon.

Laura Mamelok, Noa Rosen, Devon Halliday, Kerry Glencorse.

Brigitte Forissier, Sarah Altenloh.

Tom Haugomat.

And Mimi's, the marvelous restaurant where I sat and observed so many New Yorkers.

About the Author

With more than forty million books sold, Marc Levy is the most-read French author alive today. He's written twenty novels to date, including *The Strange Journey of Alice Pendelbury*, *The Last of the Stanfields*, *P.S. from Paris*, *Children of Freedom*, and *Replay*.

Originally written for his son, his first novel, *If Only It Were True*, was later adapted into the film *Just Like Heaven*, starring Reese Witherspoon and Mark Ruffalo. Since then, Levy has won the hearts of not only European readers; he's won over audiences around the globe. More than one and a half million copies of his books have been sold in China alone, and his novels have been published in forty-nine languages. He lives in New York City. Readers can learn more about him and follow his work at www.marclevy.info.

About the Translator

Photo © 2018 Julian Deimling

Kate Deimling translates fiction and nonfiction from French. She holds a PhD in French literature from Columbia University and wrote her dissertation on eighteenth-century libertine novels. Kate is a member of the PEN America Translation Committee and currently serves as vice president and mentoring program director of the New York Circle of Translators. She lives in Brooklyn with her family.